AN ACCIDENTAL ENCOUNTER

Annabel is on her way to work one morning after a row with her domineering mother. When she is accidentally knocked down by Garry, a policeman, her life changes forever. Soon, against her mother's advice, the two become romantically involved. Annabel has fallen in love — but her dreams are shattered by a devastating revelation. Will the couple overcome their problems and find happiness together? Or will Anna be tempted by the attentions of her boss, who she's been pining after for ages — or her handsome new neighbour?

DAWN BRIDGE

---◆---

AN ACCIDENTAL ENCOUNTER

Complete and Unabridged

LINFORD
Leicester

First published in Great Britain in 2013

First Linford Edition
published 2015

A catalogue record for this book is available
from the British Library.

ISBN 978–1–4448–2260–1

Published by
F. A. Thorpe (Publishing)
Anstey, Leicestershire

Set by Words & Graphics Ltd.
Anstey, Leicestershire
Printed and bound in Great Britain by
T. J. International Ltd., Padstow, Cornwall

This book is printed on acid-free paper

1

'Don't be late tonight, Annabel,' Maggie Barker ordered. 'I want my tea at six.'

'It's Sunday, Mum. The store doesn't close till five. You know I have to stay on for a while. There's a lot to do after all the customers have gone home. I can't just rush off.'

'I wish that supermarket didn't open on a Sunday. It never used to. Why do you have to work then? You could refuse . . . say you're . . . '

'We all have to take turns,' Annabel interrupted. 'Besides, I need the money.' She opened the fridge, took out several ingredients, placed them on the table and started buttering some slices of bread.

'But I have to eat at six, otherwise I get terrible pains in my tummy. You know I can't go long without food,' Maggie Barker whined. 'Why can't some-one else stay and do the sorting out?'

'Because I'm the supervisor; it's my job.'

'They take advantage of you at that supermarket.'

'No, they don't,' Annabel replied indignantly, jabbing the cheese with her knife.

'What about your boss? I bet he doesn't stay. Probably earns a fortune too.'

'He'll be there.' Annabel's face brightened. Her boss was just the sort of man she liked: tall, good-looking, reasonably young, and always helpful and friendly towards everyone. The problem was, he still seemed to be in mourning for his late wife. It was more than three years since her death. Annabel thought it was time he found himself someone new. How she would like to be that someone! 'Dan — er, Mr. Owen works really hard,' Annabel added.

'So he should. It's his company.'

'Yes, his father actually owns the supermarket. I think he's semi-retired

2

but Dan — Mr Owen does most of the work now.'

'I seem to remember the father would often serve in the shop years ago before they extended it. Got divorced, didn't he? I was quite shocked when I heard,' Maggie muttered. 'Divorce! That's all you hear these days. Couples don't stick together like they used to. At the first sign of trouble they split up. I suppose he's got married again. Is that right?'

'I think he has, actually, but it's none of our business.'

'I suppose not,' Maggie said grudgingly. 'Don't see his son serving in the shop though. He's too high and mighty I suppose.'

'There's so much work to do on the computer, he doesn't have time.' Annabel found herself defending Daniel Owen.

'Computers!' Maggie snorted.

'Anyway, Mum, I can't stand here talking all day. I've got to go to work. If you get really hungry, you could make the tea yourself. I've made some sandwiches for your lunch. I'll put them in the fridge, and there's cold meat and salad for tonight. You just have to wash it and put it in a dish.'

'What? With my hands? I'm surprised at you Annabel suggesting that. You've got no consideration for me. All that water . . . Washing the lettuce is really bad for them. No, I'll have to put up with the pain and wait for you to do the tea,' Maggie sighed, adopting an air of martyrdom.

Annabel groaned. She heard this every time she had to work on a Sunday. She thought it strange that her mother couldn't put her hands in water to wash the salad, but she could sit in the bath for hours! Wouldn't do anything for herself, unless she was forced to. *She wants me to wait on her hand and foot. If it's not her arthritis she's complaining about, it's her stomach.* Annabel had made her visit the doctor for a check-up, but he couldn't find anything wrong. Said it was probably because she was lonely; still suffering from grief. She needed something to keep her mind occupied. She wasn't old — not yet sixty — but she had no interest in anything except the soaps on the television and trying to run her daughter's life, Annabel thought wryly. However, her mother hadn't always been like this; only since her husband had died. He'd always spoilt and cosseted her. Now she expected her daughter to do it.

'You don't care about me,' Maggie grumbled, 'and never have. You're so selfish.'

'Me, selfish! How can you say that? I've spent the last few years looking after your every need, trying so hard to please you, but nothing I do is good enough. You're . . . so . . . so ungrateful.' Annabel flounced out of the door. How much longer could she put up with this? What should she do? If she'd had a brother or sister it might have been easier, but she'd been the only child, so all the responsibility fell on her.

She tried to escape to her bedroom but her mother followed and sat down on the bed, watching as Annabel hastily applied some face powder and lipstick. 'I don't know what you're doing that for. It doesn't improve your looks. You're no model!' she remarked. 'You're only going to work in a supermarket, not to a wedding.'

Annabel clenched her teeth, resisting the temptation to answer back. What was the point? Nothing she did would impress her mother these days. She was locked into her own world of grief and bitterness. It was almost as if she blamed her daughter for the death of her husband. Maggie had been out when Bill collapsed suddenly. Annabel had been in the house with him. She'd called the ambulance immediately but there was nothing anyone could do. The shock had affected both women in different ways. Her mother had become selfish and complaining, but Annabel had found comfort in working hard. She was good at her job and liked to keep the staff in order; after all that was what she was paid for. Sometimes she wished she could relax a little more with them, but she was frightened they'd take advantage of her. Life wasn't easy, she thought. She was approaching thirty and still living at home with her mother. At night she'd dream of meeting someone special, someone like Daniel Owen, who'd whisk her away from her drab existence. But in the morning she'd wake up to reality and more complaints from her demanding parent.

Time after time Annabel had vowed to make some changes in her life, but all had been thwarted. She'd talked of finding her own flat, but she'd received such an outcry from her mother that she'd quickly dropped that subject. She'd tried to lose weight but she'd become so frustrated with her mother's behaviour that she'd turned to comfort eating and given up her diet. *Maybe I should have left home years ago, before Dad died*, she thought. *Then Mum wouldn't have become so dependent on me and I wouldn't have been so dominated by her. I might even have been married with . . . with children.* That was something Annabel feared would never happen now. She'd spend her days looking after an ungrateful elderly mother.

'I'm off,' Annabel said, grabbing her handbag. 'Bye, Mum. I'll try not to be too late.' She hurried out of the house, ignoring her mother, who was still calling after her. As she marched down the street, all these thoughts were whirling round and round in her head. What should she do? She couldn't go on like this for much longer, putting up with her mother's ranting and raving. Life was becoming intolerable. She'd have to do something, but what?

She walked to the end of the street and started to cross the road when suddenly she felt a terrible pain in her head and left arm. Then everything went black.

A few minutes later Annabel blinked, tried to open her eyes and moaned in agony. Whatever had happened? she wondered. How did she get here? She was lying on the ground. Her head was resting on something soft. She could see people's feet around her and then someone said, 'She's coming round.'

She attempted to pull herself up, but dizziness overcame her and strong arms held her firmly. 'No, don't move. We need to get you checked out by the paramedics.'

'W . . . what happened?' Annabel stammered, trying to focus her eyes on a group of men and women who were all crowding around her. Had she fainted? No. She'd never done that in her life. She wasn't the fainting kind — too sturdily built for that — but she did feel peculiar, almost as if she were floating. Everything seemed to be spinning around her. Faces were coming and going and voices sounded muffled. 'W . . . what happened?' Annabel repeated.

'You've had a nasty accident. Don't worry, dear. You'll be all right,' a kindly voice said. 'The ambulance will be here in a minute.'

'Ambulance . . . an accident . . . how . . . ?'

'Just lie still, dear. Don't try to talk.'

Annabel couldn't do much else. The pain in her head was so bad. An accident, the woman said. She couldn't remember having an accident. Annabel closed her eyes and tried to recall what had happened. She was on her way to work, wasn't she? Then what? She couldn't think clearly. Her brain felt as if it was in a fog. Annabel gingerly attempted to move her left arm but winced in pain. Then she wriggled her right arm and gently touched her face. It felt wet and sticky. She opened her eyes and groaned. That was blood on her hand. Her face was bleeding! She moved her right arm again, touched her skirt which was covered in mud and tried to smooth it down, aware that her tights were bloodied and full of holes.

'Cover her up with this,' a female voice ordered. 'We've got to keep her warm until the ambulance gets here. She must be suffering from shock. She's very pale and she's shivering.'

A large grey coat was draped across Annabel.

'Are you feeling cold, dear?' the kindly voice asked.

'Y . . . yes.' Her teeth wouldn't stop chattering. Ooh, my head,' she groaned.

'You'll soon feel better, dear.'

Annabel's eyelids drooped. Everything was going hazy again. She could hear people moving around her, but felt too weak to watch what was going on.

'Are you all right?' Someone was tapping her shoulder.

Before she could answer a deep male voice asked, 'How is she? Has she come round yet?'

'Yes. I'm sure she'll be all right,' a woman answered. 'I don't think it's too serious.'

'Thank goodness for that. I was so worried,' the man replied.

Annabel opened her eyes and looked up at a policeman who was bending over her. 'I'm so sorry,' he said.

'Sorry?' she murmured faintly. Nothing was making sense. What had happened to her?

'I'm afraid my car hit you.'

'Your car hit me?'

'Yes, you walked into the side of it. You were crossing the road. I don't think you noticed it coming. You seemed distracted. Luckily I've got good brakes. I managed to stop quickly but I still caught your arm, and I think you must have hit your head as you fell to the ground.'

Annabel tried to think. She could remember walking down the street. She'd been on her way to work. There'd been the usual row with her mother because she was working on a Sunday. She'd crossed the road, and then everything had gone black. That must have been when the accident occurred. She hadn't seen any car and she had no recollection of being hit by one. That explained why she was covered in blood and her head was aching.

'Oh, I've . . . got to . . . to go to work,' Annabel whispered, trying to raise herself up. 'They . . . they'll be wondering where I am.'

'Lie still,' the female voice ordered. 'We mustn't move you until the ambulance gets here and the crew tell us it's safe to do so.'

'But . . . but . . . '

'Now stop worrying. You won't be going to work today. You're not fit enough for that. You'll probably need quite a few days off.'

Annabel looked at the young woman who was taking charge. She could see now that she was wearing a nurse's uniform. 'Do you remember what happened?' she asked.

'I . . . I think so. I was on my way to work, and . . . '

'Good,' the nurse replied briskly. 'I'm sure you haven't got concussion but I expect they'll keep you in hospital for a while to make sure. What's your name? I'm Jennifer. I'm a staff nurse at Glentree hospital. I was on my way home when you had your accident.'

'I'm Annabel, but only my mother calls me that. All my friends call me

Anna. My . . . my boss will be expecting me.' She could picture Daniel Owen looking at his watch and saying, 'I wonder what's happened to Miss Barker. It's not like her to be late.'

'Where do you work? We'll inform your employer for you,' the policeman told her.

'I'm the supervisor at Glentree Supermarket.'

'Okay. We'll let them know as soon as the ambulance gets here and takes you off to hospital.'

'Do I have to go?'

'Yes of course you do, to make sure you've done no permanent damage,' Jennifer spoke sharply.

'It'll be for the best,' the kindly lady who had been watching all the proceedings told her.

Suddenly Annabel started to panic. She clutched at the coat which was draped over her and tried to pull herself up. She thought of her mother at home on her own. *What's my mum going to say about this? She'll be in such a state.*

'Oh . . . oh . . . I can't stay in hospital. My mum won't be able to manage without me.'

'We'll let her know,' the policeman assured her.

'But you don't understand . . . '

'Now you just lie still. And no more talking,' Jennifer ordered. 'Getting yourself all worked up won't help.'

'Do as the nurse says, dear.' The kindly lady said. 'You're lucky she came along. This poor policeman was so upset. Thought he'd killed you, he did. He was so glad when you opened your eyes.'

'I'll find out your address from your employer,' the policeman was saying. 'I'll call round myself to let your mother know about the accident. So don't you worry, everything will be all right. You'll be better before you know it.'

Annabel lay back, exhausted, and closed her eyes. It was all very well for them to tell her not to worry, but she was worried. Her mind felt clearer now. She'd been careless and stupid, causing that accident by not concentrating on what she was doing. She didn't like letting her work colleagues down. She'd hardly had any time off since she'd been at the supermarket. Daniel relied on her to keep things running smoothly. What would happen if she had to be away for more than a few days? Who would do her job? Then there was her mother. It was probably because of her she'd had the accident. She'd been thinking about her that morning when she'd been walking to the supermarket, wondering how she could prevent the rows which occurred every time she had to work on a Sunday. *I shouldn't have let her upset me*, Annabel thought. *If I hadn't been dwelling on my problems with her I would probably have seen the car approaching.* Now her head was aching, her arm was hurting and she just wanted to sleep.

It seemed to Annabel that it was only a few seconds later when she heard the sound of an ambulance approaching and she was being poked and prodded by the crew and asked more questions. She wished everyone would leave her alone and let her sleep. Then she was carefully lifted onto a stretcher. As she lay there the policeman came over, bent down and said, 'You're going to be fine. I'll come and visit you later, see how you're getting on. Is that okay?'

Annabel sleepily opened her eyes. Nothing seemed real to her anymore. Had she been dreaming? The policeman was gazing down at her with such a look of concern on his face, waiting for an answer. What had he asked?

'Is it okay for me to visit you in hospital?' he repeated.

'Oh . . . er, all right.'

'Good. I'll see you later then. By the way, I'm Garry.'

He stood watching as the stretcher was placed in the ambulance. Annabel could see his tall, burly figure still standing there as the doors were closed. *He's quite a hunk*, she thought as she was whisked away. *Not as handsome as Daniel Owen of course, but he's certainly a good-looking man.* Suddenly she felt a lot better. Had they given her something to deaden the pain? Or was it because this attractive man was coming to see her in hospital?

2

Three hours later Annabel was sitting up in bed in the local hospital sipping a hot drink. Her left arm was still painful but the X-ray showed that nothing had been broken. The cut on her head had been glued and they'd sponged the blood from her hair. She'd been warned, however, not to wash it for a week, to allow the wound to heal. The rest of the scratches on her face and arm were superficial and would soon disappear. She wondered how bad she looked, but didn't have the energy to search for a mirror; her handbag was in the locker beside her bed.

The doctor came over to see Annabel. 'You've had a lucky escape,' he said.

'I know. I can't believe I did such a silly thing. I'm sorry I've caused so much bother. Thank you for everything.'

'I was just doing my job.' He smiled.

'I'm very pleased to say that you are going to make a full recovery.'

'Thank goodness for that.'

Although Annabel was still feeling groggy, everything was gradually coming back to her, and she could now remember what led up to the accident. She was furious with herself that her carelessness had caused it. She'd been so preoccupied thinking about her mother, she hadn't noticed the car approaching. She vowed that no matter what her mother said or did, she wouldn't allow herself to get into such a state again. Her only consolation was that things were not too bad and she would soon be better.

'Your mother has been informed of the accident and will try to visit you later,' the doctor told her. 'Your employer has also been contacted,' he added.

Everything could have been so much worse, Annabel thought. The driver of the car might have been injured and other people could have been involved. What if her injuries had been more serious? Or she'd been killed? She shuddered to think of it. She'd learn from this situation. When she felt completely better she'd plan what to do next. For the moment, she'd rest as much as possible and get her strength back. Annabel put her cup on the bedside locker and lay back against the pillows and drifted off to sleep.

A short time later she awoke to the sound of voices. She looked up and saw the policeman talking to one of the nurses. When he saw her he waved and she pulled herself up in bed, trying not to put any weight on her bad arm. *He's remembered to come*, Annabel thought, feeling her heart beginning to beat faster. She watched, smiling, as he strode over to her bed.

'Hello, Annabel. How are you?' he said formally, bending over her.

'Much better thank you. Please call me Anna. It's so nice of you to come. Why don't you sit down?' She pointed to the chair beside her bed.

'I wasn't sure if you would want to see me,' he replied, easing his huge, rugged frame onto the seat.

'Why did you think that?'

'Well, it's all my fault you're here.'

'No it isn't. I wasn't concentrating on what I was doing.'

'It's kind of you to say that, but it was my car that hit you.'

'Yes, but I should have spotted you approaching.'

'Thank you for taking it so well, Anna. I was sure you'd be angry with me.'

'No, I'm just cross with myself.'

'I called round to see your mother and explained what had happened,' Garry told her. 'She seemed very agitated about coming to see you, so I promised to fetch her this evening, if that's all right with you. She's packing a bag with some of your things — you know, nightclothes and toiletries — to make you feel a bit more comfortable.'

Visiting me is not what she's bothered about, Annabel thought. *Mum's probably wondering how she's going to manage at home without me there.* 'Yes of course you can bring her, if you don't mind,' Annabel replied looking down at the plain, sensible hospital nightdress she was wearing, thinking that she could do with some of her own things. 'I was worried about how she'd take the news,' she added.

'Your mother seemed very shocked, but I told her what the doctor said and I think I assured her you'd make a full recovery.'

'Thank you so much for everything you've done, Garry. You've been really kind. I can rest in peace now I know she's okay.' Annabel breathed a sigh of relief.

'It was the least I could do.'

'I thought the hospital was going to contact her.'

'They were, but I offered to go instead. Er . . . Anna, if you want to talk privately with your mother tonight, I'll wander off for a while and pick her up again when she's ready to go.'

'No. Don't do . . . that . . . unless you want to, of course. You can stay here.

I've nothing private to say to her. In fact I'd be glad of your support.'

Should she be saying this, Annabel wondered? After all she'd only just met this man, yet she felt as if she'd known him for ages, he was so easy to talk to. Annabel usually found it hard to make conversation with strangers, but he was different somehow. That had always been her problem, knowing what to say to people. It was probably one of the reasons why she was still single.

'My mother can be quite difficult,' Annabel continued. 'In fact sometimes she's a bit of a tyrant.'

'Okay. I'll be your chaperone.' Garry laughed. 'I suppose she'll give you a telling-off for not noticing my car. Is that it?'

'Something like that,' Anna replied.

'I've informed your boss at the supermarket too. He seems a very pleasant chap. He was most concerned about you. Said he would come and see you tomorrow evening, if that's convenient. He sent his best wishes and told you not to worry about a thing. All the staff are rallying round and they'll be able to cope.'

'Yes, he's a good boss.' Annabel replied dreamily, thinking he was a lovely man too.

'You're lucky to have a nice boss. You ought to see mine! He's huge — six feet seven inches, dwarfs me — and he's extremely bad-tempered. He frightens half the criminals into going straight, but he's a brilliant police officer.'

Annabel smiled. 'That can't be a bad thing.'

'It isn't, but all of us poor constables are terrified too!'

Annabel burst out laughing, but then clutched her head. 'Oh I mustn't do that, it makes my head ache.'

'Sorry. I'm tiring you. I'd better go now and let you get some rest.'

'Thank you again, Garry.' She leaned back against the pillows.

He stood up. 'It's time I got back to the police station, before my boss complains I've been gone too long. Got to see what crimes have been committed today.' He grinned.

He has a wonderful smile, Annabel was thinking, *and he's tall, dark and quite handsome. Just the sort of man I wanted to meet.*

'Goodbye, Anna. See you tonight at about eight. You can go back to sleep now.'

'Bye, Garry.'

Annabel snuggled down in bed. In spite of her head and arm still aching, she was feeling happier than she had for a long time. At last she was getting a break from her mother's demanding ways. If Annabel wasn't there, her mum would have to manage on her own. Maybe she'd get used to it. Tonight Garry was coming to see her and tomorrow she'd be visited by Daniel Owen. What more could a girl want? Annabel fell asleep thinking that if she had to be knocked down by someone, it couldn't have been by anyone nicer. This accident could change her life.

When Annabel awoke a few hours

later, the nurse suggested she should get up and try to walk around. 'See how you feel,' she said. 'The doctor wants to keep an eye on you. That was a nasty bump on your head. He'll probably let you go home in a couple of days though, if all goes well.'

'That's good,' Annabel replied, thinking, *Two whole days without my mother's constant complaining — just what I need!*

She eased herself out of bed and placed both feet on the cold, hard floor, hoping that her mother would remember to bring some slippers. Her elegant, high-heeled shoes which she was wearing when she'd been knocked down were stowed in the locker beside her bed. She felt too unsteady to put those on. Besides, they would look very silly with her drab cotton hospital nightgown, she mused. Annabel was surprised at how weak she felt. That accident had taken its toll. She guessed it would be some days before she'd recover completely.

Annabel crept awkwardly around the

ward, holding onto the trolleys which were positioned at the end of each bed. Her legs wouldn't move at their normal fast pace. She tried to smile at the patients who were awake and sitting up, but kept wincing when she jerked her arm. *I must look like an old woman,* she thought, *but at least I can get out of bed. Some of these poor souls look in a very bad way, and would be lucky ever to get out of bed.*

The nurse was watching her progress. 'Well done,' she called.

'It doesn't feel very good to me. My legs won't move properly,' Annabel answered breathlessly.

'They're probably stiff after the accident. Don't worry. That's to be expected. It'll take you a while to get back to normal, but you'll make it.'

'I hope so.'

'Sit down beside your bed and have a rest,' the nurse told her. 'Your dinner will be coming round soon.'

Annabel glanced at the clock on the wall. Six o'clock. Two hours until her visitors came. She wished she was wearing something more flattering than the dull nightgown. Although she was looking forward to seeing Garry again, she dreaded her mother's visit. Annabel knew she'd be in for a tongue-lashing from her.

She was surprised to find that the evening meal was quite enjoyable. It was so nice not having to cook it herself. She thought of her mother back at home eating the salad which was left in the fridge. She wondered if her mum had prepared the lettuce or decided to have something else. It would be good for her to do things. She'd been relying on Annabel too much. Perhaps this accident was a blessing in disguise. It might make her mother more self-reliant, and then . . .

Then, there was the possibility that Annabel could leave home . . . get a flat. Maybe even find a boyfriend. She closed her eyes and pictured Daniel Owen and her new policeman friend Garry. Either of these two would do.

But then reality took over. Daniel had never shown any real interest in her before, so why should he now? And Garry was probably just being polite, salving his conscience, because he'd knocked her down. An unpleasant thought suddenly struck Annabel. The chances were that Garry was married. Why hadn't that occurred to her before? She'd been daydreaming about him because he was attractive and had been friendly and kind, but that was his job. He had to be nice to people. She wasn't anything special. *So you can forget any silly ideas you might have about him*, she chided herself.

Annabel went to the bathroom to freshen up, but was horrified when she caught sight of her reflection in the mirror. There were several large scratches on her forehead, a bump on the top of her head, and her brown hair looked rather matted where the nurse had tried to clean the blood from a large cut. She'd be very glad when the week was up so she could give her hair a good wash. *I look a mess*, Annabel thought, *but there's nothing much I can do about it*. She applied a little powder and some lipstick. *That'll have to do*, she told herself.

At a few minutes after eight o'clock when Annabel was back in bed, and most patients were busy chatting to their friends and relatives, Garry walked into the ward holding the arm of her mother, who was looking very grim-faced.

'Hello, Mum,' Annabel said as Garry stood behind and her mother pecked her on the cheek.

'I can't believe you did such a stupid thing,' she sniffed. 'Getting yourself run over! You look terrible.'

'Thanks,' Annabel sighed. 'I know that. Sit down, Mum.'

'I was thinking you looked so much better,' Garry told Annabel, giving her a broad grin. 'I'll go and grab a chair. Here's some of your things.' He placed a bag on her locker.

'Thanks, Garry.'

'I hope I've thought of everything,'

Maggie muttered breathlessly.

'I'm sure you have, Mum,' Annabel replied, perusing the bag. She was thinking, *If Garry says I look better, whatever did I look like before?*

Maggie sank back into the armchair, fished around in her handbag and thrust a package at Annabel. 'I found these grapes in the fridge. Thought you might like them. You're supposed to feed grapes to invalids, aren't you?'

'Yes, I think so,' Annabel replied, trying not to smile. It was so typical of her mother that even when she was doing a kind act, she appeared grudging. 'Thanks for bringing them, Mum.'

A few moments later Garry returned and sat down next to Maggie. 'Thank you so much for bringing my mother,' Annabel said. 'It was very kind of him, wasn't it, Mum?'

'Yes, I suppose so, but you shouldn't have caused the accident. I had the fright of my life.' She glared at her daughter.

'And I didn't?' Annabel muttered

under her breath.

'What did you say?'

'Nothing.'

'Causing all that bother. Could have got yourself killed.'

'I do know that, Mum.'

'Sheer stupidity . . . that's what it was.'

'You've made your point.' Annabel closed her eyes. He head was beginning to ache again.

'Well Mrs Barker,' Garry interrupted, 'your daughter's going to make a full recovery, so let's be thankful for that. I hope we're not tiring you.'

Annabel gave him a grateful smile. 'No. My head's still a bit sore. That's all.'

'And whose fault is that?' 'Maggie snapped.

'Mine, but I've learnt my lesson. I'll be much more careful in future.'

'So you should.'

Annabel and Garry sat for the next twenty minutes making polite small talk, finding it impossible to engage Maggie in the conversation. She sat sullenly staring at both of them, finally asking, 'What am I supposed to do tomorrow for dinner?'

'Have a look in the freezer. I'm sure you'll find something you fancy.'

'I hope so. It's not full of that vegetarian muck, is it?'

'There are lots of other things too. You might even find a shepherd's pie; you could heat that up in the microwave.' Annabel thought surely this would cheer her up. It was her favourite meal.

Maggie's face brightened, but she said nothing.

The nurse rang the bell for the end of visiting time. Stiffly, Maggie got up from her chair. 'I can't promise to come and see you tomorrow,' she muttered. 'It all depends on my legs. It'll be a good thing when you're back home. If I do come, it'll have to be in the afternoon. I don't go out in the evening on my own.'

'That's okay, Mum. You look after yourself. Thanks for coming.'

Garry squeezed Annabel's hand. 'I've got to work late tomorrow evening, but I'll try and visit the next day if you're still in hospital. Let me know if they want to send you home. I'll arrange to give you a lift. That is,' he said, smiling, 'if you haven't got anyone else to fetch you and don't mind getting into the car that knocked you over.' He handed her his card. 'This is my telephone number.'

Annabel read it and placed it on her locker. She'd keep that safe. 'Thanks, Garry . . . for . . . for everything. No, there's no one else who could take me home, but I don't want to put you to any trouble; I can easily get a taxi.'

'No, I want to fetch you. If necessary they'll let me have a couple of hours off work, seeing as I was the one who knocked you down.'

'All right, that would be lovely.'

'Are we going?' Maggie grumbled. 'Can't stand here all day. You know my legs are bad.'

'Okay, Mrs Barker,' Garry replied. 'Good night, Anna. Sleep well. See you soon.'

'Anna!' Maggie exclaimed. 'Her name is Annabel.'

'All my friends call me Anna, Mum. You know that.'

'If I'd wanted you called that, you'd have been christened Anna,' she stated imperiously.

'Oh Mum.' Annabel shook her head in exasperation.

Garry winked and took hold of Maggie's arm. 'Come on, Mrs Barker. I'll give you a lift home.'

'Careful,' she muttered. 'I've got arthritis in that arm.'

'Sorry.'

Annabel waved as they walked out of the ward, reflecting that she'd never before met anyone who'd had such a big impact on her in more ways than one as this policeman had. Then picking up the card she read,

P.C. Garry Jonas.

I wonder if there's a Mrs. Jonas, she mused as she snuggled down in bed. *It would be just my luck if there is.* Eventually she fell fast asleep after mulling over the events of the day.

3

The next afternoon, Maggie huffed and puffed her way into the ward. 'I was hoping they'd have sent you home by now,' she grumbled. 'Have you got any grapes left?' She rummaged on the locker. 'I need something to refresh me after that journey here.'

'Yes, the container should be there some-where. Look inside,' Annabel answered.

Maggie found the grapes, flopped down into the armchair and sat munching them.

'I saw the doctor this morning,' Annabel continued. 'He said I should be able to go home in a couple of days.'

'Good. Let me know when you're ready. I'll arrange a taxi for you.'

'No, you don't need to do that. Er . . . Garry said he would fetch me.'

'Garry?'

'The policeman who knocked me down.'

'Oh that man! You don't want to be beholden to him.'

'Oh Mum.' Annabel smiled. 'This is the twenty-first century. I won't be beholden to him, as you put it. He just wants to help.'

'Got a guilty conscience, more like it.'

'It's no good blaming him. I should have been more careful. I walked into his car.'

'I've been thinking,' Maggie went on, ignoring her daughter's remark. 'I reckon you could sue the police for what he did. You might make some money out of it. We could do with a bit more coming in. You're not exactly well paid at the supermarket. Dangerous driving, that's what it was.'

'I'm not suing anyone. It was entirely my fault. End of discussion,' Annabel stated firmly, glaring at her mother. 'And I'm quite happy with my salary.'

Maggie tut-tutted loudly but realised she had lost the case, knowing her daughter could be as stubborn as she was. 'Anyway,' she muttered, 'I still don't understand why that policeman wants to bother with you. Probably won't come again.' An awkward silence ensued as mother and daughter sat staring at each other.

Mum always has to have the last word, Annabel was thinking, *and she never has anything good to say about me. I'm surprised, too, that Garry's being so helpful, but I can't complain about that. It's not every day a good-looking man dances attention on me. People aren't usually so kind, but I'm not going to admit that to my mother. Has he got an ulterior motive? Or is it guilt? Although he has no reason to feel guilty; I'm the one who caused the accident. I don't know what he's thinking. I'll just have to wait and see how things turn out, and meanwhile I'll just enjoy the situation. Garry said he'd come back, so I've no reason to believe he won't.*

Annabel was saved from further speculation by the arrival of Daniel

Owen. He'd come into the ward and was escorted to her bed by one of the nurses, who was smiling up at him. Annabel thought she detected a look of envy on her face. Well, he was an extremely attractive man, she mused, yet he seemed totally unaware of it.

'Hello, Annabel. This is for you.' Daniel placed a huge basket full of fruit onto the end of her bed. 'I would have brought some roses but I wasn't sure what the hospital's policy was on flowers. I know some won't let you have them.'

Annabel looked around. There didn't seem to be any. 'Thanks, Daniel. That looks delicious. I don't think they will allow flowers. It's a shame because it would brighten the place up a bit.'

'I'm sure it would. Anyway, how are you feeling, Annabel?'

'A lot better now, thank you.'

'That's good. Daniel turned to Maggie. 'Pleased to meet you again, Mrs Barker. I hope you're well.'

'Not too bad, thanks. Can't get rid of

my arthritis though. My legs are playing up today.'

'Well, I'll give you a lift home if you like.'

'How kind.'

'I'll go and find a chair,' Daniel said.

'He's nice,' Maggie whispered. 'A real gentleman. Not like that policeman. You want to play your cards right there, my girl. Roses! He was going to buy you roses. Men don't do that unless they're interested.'

'Shush, Mum,' Annabel said, blushing. 'He's a good boss. He'd do the same for any member of staff.'

'How do you know? You remember what I've said.' Maggie heaved herself up and hobbled to the end of the bed so she could see the basket of fruit better. 'That must have cost him a fortune. It's real top quality. Peaches!' she murmured. 'My favourites.'

'You can have one if you want,' Annabel told her.

'Thanks.' She grabbed a large peach from the basket, rubbed it with a tissue and proceeded to devour it.

Daniel returned with a chair and sat down opposite Maggie, whose face was dripping with juice. 'Delicious!' she exclaimed.

Daniel passed her a tissue and smiled across at Annabel. 'I'm glad your mum's enjoying it. Make sure you get some though,' he whispered.

'There's plenty for both of us,' she replied quietly. 'It's nice to see her looking happy. How's everyone at work?' she asked, changing the subject. 'I'm sorry I've caused you such a bother.'

'Now don't you worry about us,' Daniel assured her. 'We'll manage. I've asked a couple of the part-timers to put in some extra hours and Brenda's' going to help tackle your job, so everything's organised.'

Part-timers, Annabel thought. *That new woman, Jan Harvey, is probably one of them. I've noticed her going into his office a few times. Daniel always says they're discussing her hours, but*

I'm not so sure; they seem rather smiley and flirty when they're together. I've never seen him like that before. I wonder if he fancies her. After all they are a similar age, a good few years older than me. I'm sure I don't stand a chance with Daniel, whatever my mother might think. Annabel also remembered feeling rather shocked one day when Jan had mentioned her husband. She hadn't realised Jan was married and was surprised that Daniel seemed so interested in her. She couldn't imagine Daniel getting involved with someone who wasn't free.

'What do you think, Annabel?'

She blinked, suddenly realising Daniel was waiting for an answer; she hadn't heard what he'd said as she was so lost in thought. 'Sorry?'

'I was saying that our new members of staff have settled down well. Don't you agree?' Daniel asked.

'Oh, er . . . yes.'

'Are you all right, Annabel? You look a bit dazed.'

'I . . . I'm just tired.'

'Oh, we won't stay too long then.'

'No, don't rush off. I just find it hard to sleep in hospital. There's so much going on at night. I'm glad everyone's rallying round at work. I'll be back as soon as I can.'

'When the doctor says you're fit enough, and not before,' Daniel told her sternly. 'You've had a nasty shock. It'll take you a while to get over it. We don't want you having a relapse.'

'All right, I'll be a good girl.'

'That'll make a change,' Maggie sniffed.

Daniel laughed. 'You keep Annabel in order, Mrs. Barker, and don't let her come back till she's really better.'

'I'll do my best,' Maggie said, smiling, 'But she can be so stubborn.'

'I am still here,' Annabel muttered, looking from one to the other. 'I'm not deaf. I can hear you.'

'Good. I'm just trying to make you realise you've got to take things easy,' Daniel emphasised.

Now how am I going to do that?

44

Annabel was thinking. *Is my mum going to turn over a new leaf and start doing things in the house? I don't think so.*

'I'll make sure she has a rest, Mr. Owen. You leave her to me.'

Annabel nearly choked with shock. *When has my mother ever let me have a rest? She's certainly trying to make a good impression on Daniel, and he seems to be falling for it. I can't see her waiting on me for very long. I'll give it a day if I'm lucky, and then everything will be back to normal.*

'Thank you Mrs. Barker,' Daniel replied. 'I'm relying on you to look after Annabel for me.'

Thirty minutes later Annabel waved as her visitors left. *My mum should have been an actress,* she was thinking. *I've never seen her put on such an act before, pretending that she will look after me. That's not going to happen. Once I'm home she'll be back to her old ways, so I'd better make the most of my stay in hospital and enjoy the rest while I can.*

★ ★ ★

The following afternoon Maggie came on her own to visit Annabel. 'I took a taxi,' she told her. 'My legs are too bad to get the bus. That Daniel's so nice,' she cooed. 'He escorted me right to my front door yesterday. Just the sort of man I'd like for a son-in-law.'

That was the first time Annabel had heard Maggie say anything like that. She'd always believed her mother wanted her to stay single, so she wouldn't be left on her own, and she'd have someone to look after her. *I suppose she'd like to choose a husband for me. Well, it's not going to be Daniel Owen, unless a miracle happens. Anyway, I've got someone else to think about now. I hope Garry's coming to see me tonight if he doesn't have to work.*

'You'll have to smarten yourself up a bit, my girl, if you want to attract Daniel,' Maggie went on.

Smarten myself up! The cheek! Mum's always telling me she doesn't know why I bother putting on any make-up as I only work in a shop, Annabel fumed. She replied tersely, 'Oh Mum, forget Daniel. He's my boss. He's only interested in me as one of his employees.' That was probably true.

Later the same day, after her mother had gone home, a couple of checkout girls from the supermarket came to visit, carrying boxes of chocolates.

'Thank you so much! They look really scrumptious,' she exclaimed. 'I'll have to go on a diet if I eat all those.'

They laughed and one of them said, 'I hope you enjoy them. You can worry about dieting when you get home.'

They don't have to think about going on a diet; they're stick-thin, Annabel mused. *Everyone's so kind and friendly. I didn't appreciate that before. When I go back to work, I'll have to make a real effort to get on with them all. Maybe I've been a bit too bossy in the past. It's difficult though, because I am their supervisor and I need their respect, but I really will try harder to be more friendly towards them in the future.*

After the girls had gone, shortly before the end of visiting time, Garry strode across the ward. 'Sorry I'm late. I got delayed at work. Someone's gone off sick and I had to cover for them.'

Annabel smiled broadly. She was so relieved to see him. She'd begun to fear Garry wasn't going to show up. 'That's all right. Thank you for coming.'

'I had to see how you were.'

They sat chatting and laughing until the nurse rang the bell for the end of visiting time. Annabel had spotted the nurse glaring over at them a couple of times. 'You'll be thrown out of here in a minute if you keep making me laugh.'

'Just trying to cheer you up,' Garry replied, breaking forth into another rendering of 'A Policeman's Lot Is Not a Happy One.'

Annabel was doubled up with laughter as Garry tried to reach the bottom notes. 'Stop it,' she begged. 'You'll be accused of disturbing the other patients.'

'Laughter is the best medicine, they say.'

He glanced around the ward. 'It looks as if that's what some of this lot need.'

'Maybe, but the nursing staff might not agree with you.'

'Okay, I'll leave you in peace now. Good night, Anna; sleep well. I'll see you soon. Let me know if you need my help.'

★ ★ ★

Three days later Garry took Annabel home from hospital. He'd dropped her off at her house and then had to hurry back to the police station. She'd contacted him as soon as she knew she was being discharged. Then she told her mother that everything had been arranged and Garry was bringing her home.

'We could have got a taxi,' Maggie grumbled when Annabel walked into the house. 'You didn't need to get that policeman to do it. You're becoming too involved with him, if you ask me.'

'I'm not asking you,' Annabel mumbled, thinking, *Normally my mother would*

49

never suggest getting a taxi. Far too expensive she'd say, but because Garry had offered to fetch her she had to take the opposite view. Annabel couldn't understand why her mother was so opposed to Garry, yet she liked Daniel Owen. *I suppose she considers being the manager of a supermarket is a better job than being a police constable. Or, maybe she's jealous of all the attention Garry's giving me.*

'You could have got Daniel Owen to bring you home,' Maggie continued, 'if you didn't want to spend money on a taxi. You missed your chance there, my girl.'

Annabel clenched her teeth. Now her mum was making it seem as if she was the one who was too mean to get a taxi. 'Daniel's my boss and he's a very busy man. There was no need to bother him,' she snapped. 'Garry had said he'd do it. He was able to pick me up between shifts.'

'All you talk about these days is Garry this and Garry that,' Maggie grumbled.

'He ran you over. Have you forgotten that?'

'I walked into his car,' Annabel said wearily. 'Can we please change the subject? I'd love a cup of tea, please, Mum.'

'Oh, all right,' Maggie replied grudgingly. 'I'll put the kettle on. We've got beans on toast tonight. I didn't have time to get anything else in.'

'That's fine.'

'Well, now you're back here, we won't see any more of that policeman I hope,' Maggie muttered. 'He'll soon forget about what he did to you, now he's cleared his conscience by bringing you home.

'Sorry Mum,' Annabel said with glee, 'But Garry's coming round tomorrow evening when he's finished his shift.'

'Oh no! Why did you have to invite him?'

'He said he wanted to see me again.'

'Well, don't make a regular habit of it.'

'I can have my friends round whenever I want,' Annabel stated firmly. 'I'm not a child. We won't disturb you. We'll go into the front room. You can still watch your soaps.'

'Don't go all hoity-toity with me, my girl, just because some man's looked at you twice. He'll be nothing but trouble. You mark my words.' Maggie glared at her daughter. 'Now, if it was Daniel Owen coming round, that'd be a different matter. He's a real gentleman.'

'And Garry's not? Is that what you think?'

'I'm not going to argue with you. There's no point when you're in that mood. I'll put the kettle on.' Maggie stomped out of the room.

Ooh my mother's impossible, Annabel thought. *As soon as I'm fit enough I really will look into finding my own flat. It's time I did it. I can't stay here forever.*

* * *

The next day, as Annabel's head had healed quite well, she was able to wash her hair for the first time since the accident. She found it tricky to do, as her arm was still extremely painful, but she wanted to look her best for Garry. When it was dry she smoothed her hair and tied it back into her usual ponytail, fastening it with a band that matched her dress. Then she carefully applied some make-up.

'You're not getting yourself all tarted up for that . . . that . . . plodding policeman, are you?' Maggie asked. 'You're wasting your time there. He's probably got a girlfriend already, or worse still, a . . . a wife. Nothing'll ever come of it.'

Annabel bit her tongue and kept quiet. This was not the time to get herself in a state over her mother. Maybe nothing would come of it, but for the moment she'd enjoy it. At last she'd met a man who seemed to be genuinely interested in her and she wasn't going to let her mother spoil things.

By the time Garry arrived, Maggie was ensconced in the lounge watching her favourite soap. Annabel showed him into the front room and went into the kitchen to make some coffee. When she returned they sat opposite one another, chatting and drinking. Suddenly Garry came over to her and said, 'Why don't you let your hair go loose, Anna? I want to see what it looks like.'

'I . . . I always tie it back. It's better for work.'

'But you're not at work now. Please let me see. May I?'

Garry reached down and gently unfastened Annabel's ponytail. 'There, that's better. You have lovely hair, but no one can see it when it's tied back.'

Annabel blushed. Was she hearing right? Garry had called her unruly brown hair lovely, and he was gazing at her as if he'd never seen her before. She caught sight of her reflection in the mirror over the mantelpiece and she, too, hardly recognised the radiant face surrounded by a halo of shining, chestnut curls.

'I think I'll call you Belle. My Belle,

because you . . . you look so . . . so beautiful.'

Garry was stroking her hair tenderly and she was gazing up at him when the door was thrust open. They sprang apart like two guilty children.

'They've changed the programme,' Maggie complained. Then she noticed her daughter's hair. 'Annabel, what have you done to yourself?' she shrieked. 'You look ridiculous. Go and tie your hair back at once. And you can make me a drink too. I see you've made one for yourselves. I'm worn out with all the work I've done today, all that housework and then cooking the dinner. You could have asked me if I wanted one. That's not too much trouble, is it?' She slumped down into an armchair and glared at them.

'I like Anna's hair,' Garry said. 'Don't speak to her like that. She's not a child.'

'How dare you tell me what to do!' Maggie shouted. 'Who do you think you are? And don't call my daughter

Anna. I told you that before.'

'I . . . I'm so sorry Garry,' Annabel murmured, close to tears. 'I . . . I think it might be better if you leave now. I'll sort things out with my mother.'

'Are you sure that's what you want? You should stand up to her more.'

'I know, but now's not the time. I . . . I don't feel up to it.'

'Oh, I understand, Anna — er, Annabel. Yes I'll go, but I'll be in touch soon.' He turned to Maggie. 'Good night, Mrs. Barker. If I were you I'd try to calm down. Getting in a state is not good for your blood pressure.'

'Goodbye, and don't bother coming back!' Maggie yelled.

Garry followed Annabel to the door. He bent down, lightly kissed her forehead and whispered, 'Good night, my Belle.'

4

Two days after her mother had been rude to Garry, Annabel still hadn't heard from him. She decided to ring his mobile but was disappointed when there was no reply. She guessed he was working late. He'd explained that he often had to do overtime. Annabel left a message apologising for her mother's bad behaviour, hoping that he wasn't annoyed with her.

Annabel had reprimanded Maggie about her treatment of Garry but she wouldn't listen. 'We don't want him coming round all hours. Liberty-taker, he is; makes himself too comfortable here. He's a bad influence on you. You've enough airs and graces without him making it worse. Telling you to wear your hair loose, indeed! You looked a right hussy!'

Annabel walked away as Maggie

continued complaining. She didn't try to defend herself or Garry. She knew there was no point in doing so. When her mother was in that sort of mood she never listened to reason. Annabel had hoped that after the accident her mum would mellow a bit, but once her daughter had been home a couple of days and was improving, Maggie was back to her old ways. All her promises to Daniel Owen about looking after Annabel had been in vain, as she'd suspected they would be.

If only I'd left home years ago, Annabel thought once more. *Then a vague notion went through her head. Maybe I still could. Mum's not an old woman. She doesn't need looking after. There's nothing wrong with her, apart from slight arthritis. If I found myself a flat she'd have to manage. I could ask Garry to help me look. Then we'd be able to spend time together without my mother as a chaperone. That is, of course, if Garry still wants to see me.* Annabel kept remembering he'd called her beautiful and had kissed her as he'd left. No one had ever done that before. Annabel had not thought of herself as attractive; her mother had always denigrated her so much that she'd believed her mum was right. All this was a new experience for Annabel and she was enjoying it. She even felt different, more confident somehow. Was Garry interested in her, or did he say the same thing to other women? He must meet plenty of those in his job, she mused.

Annabel decided to visit her colleagues at the supermarket. She thought Sunday morning would be a good time as there were usually fewer customers then. The doctor had given her permission to return to work the following week with the proviso that she wouldn't do too much. 'You must learn the art of delegation,' he'd said. 'I know you're a bit of a workaholic. The supermarket's survived without you. It hasn't fallen down. So make sure you take things gently.'

'I will,' Annabel promised. 'I still get tired quite quickly.' The accident had left her feeling weak and vulnerable. She'd have to gradually ease herself back into the job.

Maggie was watching the Sunday service on television when Annabel set off for the supermarket. Annabel had left her hair loose and put on a new pale blue, frilly crêpe blouse and black, slinky skirt. She was pleased that the scar at the side of her face was healing nicely, and was almost invisible now her hair was left untied. Her arm, too, felt much better. *I'll give them all a surprise when they see the new me*, she thought.

She called, 'Bye,' and hurried out of the door before her mum could make any demands. Annabel could hear her speaking but pretended she hadn't.

She'd had one brief message from Garry the day before saying, 'Working on a very important case; will be in touch soon. Garry.'

He had warned her that sometimes he'd find it difficult to contact her because of his job, so she wasn't too concerned that she hadn't seen him since the night her mother was rude and aggressive. She was reassured that he still wanted to see her.

She'd heard on the news that there'd been a threat to kidnap the wife of a senior member of the local council and all police leave had been cancelled. The woman had been too outspoken and had offended some members of a minority group. A journalist had got hold of the story and published it in their local paper. It said that she was being given round-the-clock police protection until the culprits were caught, so Annabel guessed this would affect Garry.

When Annabel walked into the supermarket, the first person she saw was Brenda. 'You look lovely,' she gasped. 'Your hair really suits you like that, and that blouse . . . it's so pretty.'

'Thank you,' Annabel mumbled, her face flushed. She wasn't used to receiving compliments and felt rather embarrassed. 'How's everything?'

'We're coping, but missing you of course. How are you? You look so well.

When are you coming back?'

'Next week. I feel much better, thanks.'

'Good. I'm sure Daniel will be pleased to see you. He's had to put up with me trying to do your job, but I'm not as efficient as you.'

'I'm sure you are. Where is Daniel? Is he in today?' Annabel looked around.

'He's in his office,' I think,' Brenda informed her.

'I'll go and say hello.'

As Annabel walked along, her mobile phone sounded. There was a brief text from Garry: 'Work still hectic. All leave cancelled. Hope you are okay. Will ring soon. Love, Garry.'

Now she felt even happier. He was thinking about her and best of all he'd ended the text, 'Love, Garry'.

On the way to Daniel's office Annabel stopped off to talk to some of the checkout girls. They all seemed pleased to see her and commented favourably on her appearance. *I'm beginning to look forward to coming back to work*, Annabel was thinking as she tapped on Daniel's door.

'Come in,' he called.

As she entered he gazed at her in astonishment. 'Annabel, you . . . you look wonderful.'

'Thank you,' she mumbled, her face reddening. All this praise was going to her head. It was amazing what a new hairstyle could do for one's confidence, she thought.

'How's your arm? You certainly look better,' Daniel was saying as he gazed at Annabel as if he were seeing her for the first time.

'Oh, I'm getting on really well, thanks. I'll be returning to work next week.'

'That's marvellous. We've all missed you. It's been a struggle but Brenda's done her best. I think she'll be glad to get back to her old routine, though.'

They chatted for a few more minutes. Then Annabel left the supermarket and went home. She crept upstairs before her mother could see her, changed into something more casual and tied back her hair. She didn't want any difficult confrontations over her appearance. She and her mother would never see eye to eye.

'About time too,' her mother muttered as Annabel walked into the lounge. 'I'm starving.'

'You could have got the lunch ready. You didn't have to wait for me.'

'I wasn't sure what you wanted. Anyway, my arthritis is bad today. You're up and about now, so I thought you'd be getting it, like you always used to.'

'All right, I'll sort something out,' Annabel answered. She was feeling cheerful and wasn't going to let her mother upset her.

'When are you going back to work?'

'Next week.'

'I bet they'll be glad to see you.'

'I think they will.'

'Maybe your boss will give you a rise. I'm sure you deserve one.'

'Oh Mum, that's all you ever think of — money!'

'Well we're not exactly rich, are we?

Did you see Daniel Owen today?'

'Yes, I saw him.'

'What did he say?'

'That he was pleased I was getting better and would be coming back to work next week.' Annabel didn't tell her mother about the look of admiration she'd seen on Daniel's face. Some weeks earlier, she mused, she would have been delighted about that, but these days she was far more interested in Garry than her boss.

* * *

The following week Annabel returned to work. She still hadn't seen Garry but she'd had a couple of texts from him stating that he was looking forward to seeing her again when things got back to normal at the station. She'd read in the paper that the police were following up several leads and hoped that an arrest was imminent.

'That Garry hasn't been around recently,' Maggie remarked one day. 'A good thing too, if you ask me.'

'I'm not asking,' Annabel muttered.

'I told you he'd soon lose interest once he knew you weren't going to sue him,' Maggie continued. 'I know the type. He was just acting all nice and friendly so you wouldn't take action against him, and you fell for it.'

'You don't know what you're talking about.' Annabel flounced off. She hoped her mother was wrong, but she too was beginning to have doubts about Garry. It was so long since she'd seen him. She wanted to believe what he'd said, but as the time passed she couldn't help wondering if he really was interested in her. Could her mother be right?

One evening Annabel staggered home from the supermarket, feeling exhausted. She was finding going back to work more tiring than she'd expected. She just wanted to have her dinner and crawl into bed, but her mother was up to her old tricks again.

'I'm starving,' she grumbled as Annabel tottered through the front door. 'Keeping me waiting like this is not good enough. You know I need my food regularly.'

'I'm tired, Mum. Couldn't you have put the oven on? I told you this morning, there's a casserole in the fridge. It just needs heating. I'm going to sit down for half an hour.'

'My legs ache,' Maggie whined.

'So do mine,' Annabel muttered, throwing off her shoes and rubbing her feet as she slumped down onto the sofa. She'd got out of the habit of wearing high heels after the accident. 'I've been on them all day, not like some people who've nothing better to do than sit around watching television for hours.'

'My arms ache and my neck's stiff too,' Maggie complained. 'You don't care about my arthritis. You're so selfish, Annabel. That's what you are. Leaving me all day on my own, expecting me to get dinner ready. I want it now. You can have a rest afterwards.'

'Look, Mum.' Annabel's voice was terse. 'I have to go to work. We need the money, as you keep reminding me. You're quite capable of going to the fridge, taking the casserole out, putting it in the oven and switching it on.'

'Don't order me around. I'm your mother.'

'How could I ever forget?' Annabel muttered, getting up. 'I'm going to my bedroom for a bit of peace and quiet. Call me when the dinner's ready.' She felt too weary to argue any more. Annabel could still hear her mother grumbling as she clambered up the stairs. She entered her room, locked the door and collapsed onto the bed. Within a few moments she had fallen into a deep sleep.

Forty minutes later Annabel was awakened by the sound of someone banging on her door. 'Go away,' she murmured sleepily.

'Annabel,' her mother yelled. 'I've put the oven on. If you come down now we can have our dinner. I'll dish it up. I'm faint with hunger.'

'All right,' Annabel called, smiling.

Her mother, like her, was not the fainting kind. They were both too sturdily built for that. *At least Mum's doing something*, she thought. *Maybe because I've been so soft with her in the past, giving in to her wiles too easily, that's why she treats me like a slave. I'll have to take a firmer line in the future*, Annabel resolved.

They were halfway through their meal when Maggie remarked, 'There was a phone call for you when you were asleep.'

'Who was it?' Annabel felt her heart beating faster. She put down her knife and looked up. Could it have been Garry? she wondered.

'How do I know?'

'Didn't you ask?'

'Couldn't understand what they were saying.'

'Was it a man or a woman?' Annabel was becoming impatient.

'A man.'

'You didn't recognise the voice?'

'Well,' Maggie hesitated, 'could have been that Garry I suppose. Anyway, whoever it was, I told them not to bother us any more.'

'You what?' Annabel shrieked, jumping up from the table. 'How . . . how dare you? Meddling in my affairs.' She was beside herself with rage now. 'You . . . you interfering old . . . '

'Don't speak to me like that!' Maggie interrupted, glaring at her daughter.

'I'll speak any way I want.' Annabel flounced from the room. She grabbed her mobile phone from the bag where she'd left it when she returned from work. Why did Garry have to ring the house phone? She'd tell him in future just to ring her mobile. She looked down at it and realised it needed re-charging. If only she'd noticed that before. She took it up to her bedroom and plugged it in. Then she crept downstairs to the hall and dialled Garry's number.

He answered the phone immediately. 'Hello, Annabel. Nice to hear your voice at last. I kept ringing your mobile but couldn't get you, so I tried your land line.'

'It needed recharging. I . . . I'm so sorry about my mother,' Annabel said in a small voice. She . . . she's impossible.'

'Don't worry about it. I know she gives you a hard time. For some reason she seems to have taken a dislike to me. I'll have to try and win her round.'

'I . . . I thought you might be upset . . . '

'No. I'm quite thick-skinned, you know. Policemen have to be,' he laughed.

'Yes . . . I suppose they do. I've never really thought of that.'

'With all those criminals trying to get at us, calling us names amongst many other things which I won't mention. Anyway, I'll let you know as soon as I get some free time. This case at work is turning out to be very tricky. All leave has been cancelled until it's solved. It's a real pain. I've missed you, Anna.'

'I've missed you too, Garry. Very much.'

'Maybe with a bit of luck I'll be able to see you next week. We're following up a new lead now.'

'I do hope so,' Annabel breathed, thinking it must be the kidnapping case Garry was working on. It was still in the newspapers. They had apprehended one of the offenders who had threatened to abduct the councillor's wife, but another was still on the loose.

'I'll arrange it somehow. I can't wait much longer. I keep looking at that gorgeous picture I took of you.'

'Oh Garry,' Annabel sighed, blushing. She was remembering when he'd taken that picture on his mobile phone. Her hair had been loose and flowing and he'd stroked it so tenderly, until her mother had burst in on them and spoilt everything. 'I can't wait either,' she told Garry.

'Bye my Belle,' he said. 'See you soon.'

Annabel hung up, feeling much better. Garry was still interested. Her mother's dire warnings were just the meaningless ramblings of an old, jealous woman, she guessed.

'Who were you ringing?' Maggie

enquired as she walked into the lounge. 'Not that policeman, I hope?'

'Just a friend,' Annabel replied, resisting the temptation to answer back. She was feeling cheered up by her chat with Garry and wasn't going to let her mother ruin her mood.

★ ★ ★

Two days later Annabel approached the local estate agent and discovered that there were several flats in the neighbourhood which she could afford to rent. She made appointments to view two of them but didn't tell her mum. Since the incident with Garry, Annabel and her mother had settled for an uneasy truce. They mostly only communicated with each other when they had to, but Annabel had noticed that Maggie was making some effort to do more in the house. This was reassuring to Annabel. She knew her mother would be able to cope on her own. She wasn't incapacitated. Many people were much more badly affected by arthritis than she was. It might even be good for her to look after herself.

Garry sent a text saying he would see Annabel at the weekend and would be in touch nearer the time to make arrangements. He ended the message as before: 'Love, from Garry.' Did he mean that, Annabel wondered, or were they just words he used at the end of all his texts?

She replied, 'Can't wait to see you. Love, from Anna.'

She did mean that.

* * *

Annabel went to view the flats. One was on the ground floor and was not as nice as it looked in the picture. The other was on the first floor of a three-storey block surrounded by attractive gardens. She thought it was very pleasant, and not too far away from her mother's house and the supermarket. It had two bedrooms, a large lounge, a modern fitted kitchen and a balcony. It was unfurnished and would be available in two weeks.

Annabel looked around, picturing what furniture she would put in it, wondering what it would be like living on her own. She also imagined Garry visiting her there. She'd never seen where he lived. After the accident she hadn't been able to get around. She knew his address. It was the other side of the town. He'd said it was a one-bedroom flat, compact, yet had everything he needed. Once she'd moved into hers they'd be able to visit each other. They'd be free from her mother's endless complaints and criticisms.

Annabel decided to put a deposit on the flat at once to secure it. It was too good an opportunity to miss. The only thing worrying her now was how she was going to break the news to her mother.

5

Two days later, Garry rang Annabel and suggested they go to a concert at the local college.

'I've definitely got Saturday off,' he told her. 'My boss promised me that, as I've had no leave for a couple of weeks.'

'How's the case going? Or are you still not allowed to say anything?'

'Well, I can tell you that with a bit of luck we'll soon have it tied up. We've been following several leads and I think we're onto a winner.'

'That's good.'

'What about the concert, Anna? Do you want to go?'

'Yes, I'd love to. I believe the students are excellent — not that I've been to their concerts very often.'

'I haven't either, but I've heard their conductor is brilliant.'

'What's the programme?'

'I can't remember, but it's probably something quite light. I'm sure we'll enjoy it. That's a date then. Bye, my Belle.'

Annabel couldn't wait for Saturday to come. She didn't tell her mother she'd heard from Garry again. She couldn't face having any more rows with her. Instead, she decided she'd just say she was going out with a friend. Then, when Garry arrived to pick her up, she'd hurry out of the door before her mother could see who was there.

Annabel got up very early the morning of the concert. She prepared two plates of ham and egg salad and made a fruit jelly. 'We can have this tonight when I come home from the supermarket,' she told Maggie.

'What about my lunch?' her mother enquired.

'I've left you a dish of pasta. You just have to heat it up in the microwave.'

'Thanks,' Maggie muttered grudgingly.

What an ungrateful old . . . woman!

She's never satisfied with anything I do, Annabel thought as she picked up a pile of DVDs and held them out to her mother. 'I was tidying my bedroom last night when I came across these. I thought you might be interested in seeing them before I take them to the charity shop.' She passed them to Maggie, who studied the titles. Gradually a smile broke out across her face.

'Ooh, thanks, Annabel. My favourites! I might watch them tonight. There's nothing worth seeing on the television. Too much sport these days.'

'Okay, Mum. I'm off now. Bye.'

Annabel walked out of the house feeling pleased with herself. So far everything was going to plan.

* * *

When Garry rang the doorbell that evening, Maggie was seated in the lounge in her favourite armchair, watching television with a box of chocolates beside her. She'd hardly paid any attention to

Annabel as she got ready for her date.

'I'm just coming,' she whispered to Garry as he gave her a brief kiss on the cheek.

'See you later, Mum. I'm off now,' Annabel called without going into the lounge. She didn't want any criticisms about her appearance or hairstyle. She'd left her hair loose and was wearing a new blue dress which fitted her perfectly. She'd been delighted that since recovering from the accident, she'd lost a few more pounds and had gone down a dress size.

'You're getting too skinny,' her mother had complained one day.

Annabel had laughed. 'I don't think so,' she'd replied, feeling pleased. She guessed that Maggie was jealous, as she now had a rather ample figure.

'Don't be late,' Maggie answered.

'I won't,' Annabel assured her, still without going into the lounge. 'But if you want to go to bed, you don't have to wait up for me.'

As she walked out of the door she

could hear her mother yelling, 'Who are you going out with?'

Annabel pretended she hadn't heard and closed the front door.

Garry put his arm around her and said, 'I'm so pleased to see you, Anna. It's been a long time. You look lovely tonight.'

'Thank you. I'm pleased to see you too,' she murmured. He took her hand and led her to his car.

Soon they were seated upstairs in the grand hall, waiting for the concert to begin. Annabel looked around, feeling very content. A few weeks ago she would never have imagined that she would be sitting here at this concert with a very attractive policeman as her escort. Suddenly she spotted Daniel Owen downstairs making his way along a row. 'There's my boss,' she told Garry excitedly, pointing to a tall man dressed in a smart dark suit. 'I didn't know he was going to be here. Oh, he's got someone with him,' she exclaimed.

'It's probably his wife,' Garry replied,

looking at Annabel quizzically.

'No. He's a widower. His wife died three years ago. He's been mourning her ever since.'

'You seem to know a lot about him.'

'Well, I have worked for Daniel a long time, and as far as I know he's never even looked at another woman, he was so devastated by his wife's death.' She knew that from personal experience. How many times in the past had she wished Daniel would notice her?

'Then it's time he found himself someone else, so it's probably his girlfriend.' Garry smiled.

'What are you grinning about?' Annabel asked.

'I'm just thinking that you don't know much about men if you believe he's never even looked at another woman.'

'Oh.' Annabel could feel her face flushing. 'I . . . I . . . er, just mean that . . . he . . . '

'It's all right. I know what you mean. I was only teasing,' Garry laughed. 'I've got the message. Your boss was really devoted to his wife. Now are we going to spend the whole evening talking about him?'

'No, of course not. Sorry.' Annabel was flustered. Garry must think that she was very naïve. She'd have to pull herself together. Seeing Daniel at the concert with a very attractive and some-what younger woman in tow had unnerved her. But why shouldn't he be there with somebody, she reasoned. After all, she was with Garry. Anyway, why waste the evening speculating about Daniel, a man who was not interested in her, when she was dating a gorgeous policeman?

There was no time for further talk as the lights dimmed and the orchestra started up. From time to time Annabel glanced at Garry, who seemed to be absorbed in the music. After the over-ture, he whispered, 'Are you enjoying it, Anna?'

'Yes, thank you. The orchestra's brilliant,' she replied. 'I'm so glad we've come.'

'Good.' As the music started again

Garry took hold of her hand, only releasing it when the work ended and the audience had to applaud. Annabel sat still, feeling so happy. She wondered what her mother would think if she could see her now.

During the interval Garry took her to the coffee bar which was just outside the grand hall. As they were queuing up, Daniel and his escort came past. He noticed Annabel straight away and steered his partner over to her.

'Hello, Annabel. How nice to see you. May I introduce you to my . . . my friend Olivia.'

After the introductions, Daniel said, 'The orchestra are very good, aren't they? I'd forgotten how professional they sound. It's hard to believe they're just students.'

'Yes, they're brilliant, but they are all studying music, I think,' Garry answered.

'That's right. It tells you about them in the programme,' Daniel affirmed.

'They're as good as anything I've heard in the States, or anywhere else,' Olivia added.

Daniel turned to her and said, 'I think we'd better join the end of the queue, otherwise we'll be too late to get a drink. Please excuse us. Enjoy the rest of the concert, you two.'

Annabel noticed Garry was staring after them as they walked away. She felt quite dowdy in comparison to Daniel's dazzling escort. If that was the sort of woman he was attracted to, it wasn't surprising he'd never shown any interest in her. She couldn't compete with someone like that. 'Olivia's rather glamorous isn't she?' Annabel said quietly.

'Yes I suppose she is,' Garry replied.

'Do you think she's American?'

'Could be. She has a slight American twang.'

'I wonder how he met her.'

'I don't know and I really don't care, Anna. Can we please discuss something other than your boss? I'm beginning to think you're more interested in him than me.'

'Oh. Sorry, Garry.' She patted his arm. 'Of course I'm not.' Annabel thought, *I might have been at one time, but not anymore.* 'I . . . I'm just rather curious about him.'

'So I've noticed. Now what do you want to drink?'

For the remainder of the concert Annabel refrained from mentioning Daniel, but from time to time she couldn't stop herself wondering about Olivia. Annabel felt rather protective towards Daniel and hoped that this young woman would treat him well. After all, she thought, he was her boss and she had known him for many years, both before and after he'd been widowed.

During the second half of the concert Garry took hold of Annabel's hand and she sat back, enjoying the music and being with him. *Is Daniel holding Olivia's hand?* she mused. Then, when the audience applauded each work and she joined in enthusiastically, Garry smiled at her and she forgot all about Daniel.

'That was the best concert I have ever been to,' she murmured as they were walking out of the hall.

'Yes, it was very good,' Garry agreed.

On their way home, Annabel informed him that she'd put a deposit on a flat.

'Good for you. Have you told your mother?' he asked.

'No, I haven't.'

'She's not going to be very happy, is she?'

'That's putting it mildly! I dread telling her.'

'Would you like me to be with you when you do? You might need some moral support.'

'No, I think it's better if I do it on my own, otherwise she . . . she'll think that you've influenced me.'

Garry laughed. 'Yes, she'll blame me for leading you astray, I expect.'

Annabel thought that was probably what she would say, but she didn't tell Garry that.

When they arrived back at Annabel's house, they stood outside talking for a few moments. Then Garry pulled her close, stroked her hair and kissed her gently on the lips. 'Good night, my Belle,' he whispered. 'I'll see you very soon.'

Annabel was pleased that her mother was in bed when she entered the house. She felt on cloud nine. Everything was wonderful. It wouldn't be long before she had her own flat, and then she and Garry would be able to spend more time together. Even the thought of telling her mother that she was moving out couldn't dampen her spirits.

That night she hardly slept. She kept thinking, *Can this really be happening?* All the events of the evening were re-playing in her head, especially the last few minutes when Garry had kissed her.

The next morning he rang her mobile briefly and asked if she'd like to go to an engagement party with him the following Saturday.

'I'd love to,' she replied. This would give her the opportunity to meet some of Garry's friends from the police force.

'Of course,' he warned her, 'If some

new big case crops up, I might have to cancel, but I'm hopeful that won't happen.'

Annabel was an optimist that week and couldn't believe anything would go wrong. She went shopping and bought herself a new dress to wear for the party. It was turquoise silk, similar to the outfit Olivia was wearing at the concert. She'd noticed Garry gazing admiringly at her trim figure in the slinky dress. She knew she couldn't compete with Olivia — she was much too solidly built — but she was pleased that her diet had worked and she'd managed to lose a few more pounds.

Maggie had commented on Annabel's appearance once again. 'What's wrong with you? You've lost more weight.'

'Good. That's what I need to do.'

'You're not pining over that Garry, are you? Forget him. He's not worth it.'

Annabel ignored her mother's remark. She wasn't going to be provoked. Maggie didn't know that she'd seen Garry the previous week. She also still hadn't been told about the flat. *I'll just inform her a couple of days before I move out,* Annabel decided. *That way there'll be less time for her to make a fuss.*

At last, the day of the party arrived. Garry had texted her to say he'd definitely got the evening off and he'd collect her at eight thirty. Annabel hadn't told any of her work colleagues about the party, in case Garry had to work and they'd been unable to go.

He arrived precisely on time. Maggie was watching a soap and hadn't witnessed any of Annabel's preparations. 'Bye, Mum,' she called. 'Don't wait up.' She hurried out of the door before her mother could start any of her delaying tactics.

'You look wonderful,' Garry whistled, squeezing her hand.

Annabel felt wonderful. She glided along beside him, feeling as if she were in a dream. *This is going to be the best evening of my life*, she thought. She could see the future stretching out in front of her, getting better and better.

Garry's friends were all very pleasant and friendly, especially the couple whose party it was. 'We'll have to go out as a foursome,' they suggested.

'That would be lovely,' they both agreed.

Annabel and Garry sat chatting and watching the couples who were dancing. 'Do you want to have a go?' he asked at one point.

'I'm not very good,' she confessed.

'Neither am I,' he replied. 'I have two left feet, but I don't mind trying if you're game.'

'Okay.'

They got up onto the dance floor and fell about laughing at their rather feeble attempts at dancing. When they were feeling tired they sat down and Garry brought Annabel a glass of champagne. 'I'll just have a sip,' he told her. I've got to drive home.'

'Yes,' she laughed, 'we can't have a policeman getting drunk in charge of a car. This will be an evening I'll always remember,' she whispered to Garry.

* * *

That night as she lay in bed heart-broken, crying into her pillow unable to sleep, Annabel thought it had indeed been a memorable evening, but for all the wrong reasons. It was one she wanted to forget, but probably never would. How could an evening which had started with so much promise end in such disaster?

6

Annabel was still in a state of shock several days after that fateful engagement party. It had started so well, she'd never imagined anything ruining it, especially something so awful. But when she'd calmed down, she told herself she should have realised that it was all too good to be true. Life didn't go smoothly for her. Other girls seemed to jog along without anything bad happening to them. They'd go out, meet someone and live happily ever after. Now that prospect seemed unlikely for her.

Annabel wondered how she could have been so naïve as to think that she and Garry had a future together. He hadn't promised anything, but she was so inexperienced that she'd been foolish enough to trust him and believed that his feelings for her were the same as those she had for him. When he'd kissed her, she had thought it meant something, but now she knew she'd been wrong. Annabel guessed Garry had done that to lots of other girls, but they'd probably been more worldly wise than her and not taken it so seriously. They'd just enjoyed a bit of flirting and fun with him, but she couldn't be like that.

Garry had made Annabel feel special, but now she knew that was what he did to anyone he was involved with. Other more experienced young women wouldn't have been taken in by him as she had. Annabel vowed that would not happen again. In future she'd be more restrained with her feelings and less trusting.

Garry rang Annabel every day after the party but she ignored his calls. At first he tried her mobile, and then eventually her home telephone. By then Annabel had instructed her mother that if she answered one of his calls she was to hang up immediately.

'Have you finished with him, Annabel? I told you he was up to no good,' she gloated. What's he done?'

'I don't want to talk about it,' she replied, biting back the tears which threatened to come.

Maggie kept quiet for a while after that. Annabel guessed it was because she was pleased something had come between them. For once her mother was shrewd enough to say no more in case Annabel started to defend Garry and forgive him. That was not going to happen, Annabel thought. She was sure that she would never forgive him and even if she did, nothing could ever come of their relationship. It was over and would stay that way.

At night when she was trying to get to sleep, Annabel continually replayed the events of that dreadful evening in her head. She'd been fortunate that when she'd arrived home after the party, her mother had been in bed asleep. She was a very heavy sleeper and hadn't heard a thing. Annabel had rushed into her bedroom, threw herself down onto the bed and sobbed into her pillow for what seemed like hours. She worked herself into such a state that she was actually physically sick.

She'd already arranged to have the next day off work, which was a good thing as she would not have been fit enough to go in. She'd expected to be at home recovering from a night's over-indulgence and merriment, not to be nursing a broken heart. Annabel felt the staff at the supermarket had been very good to her concerning the time she'd had off because of the accident and she didn't want to let them down.

When Annabel heard her mother get up, she crawled downstairs to inform her that she'd eaten something which had disagreed with her and wouldn't be able to make breakfast as usual.

'I suppose I'll have to get it myself,' Maggie sniffed. 'What was it you ate? Prawns? They always make me sick.'

'I don't know.'

'Or did you have too much to drink? Has that Garry been leading you into bad ways? I suppose it was him who took you to the party? And I guess he was the one who kept ringing your mobile earlier while you were still asleep? You shouldn't go to these parties. They give you all sorts of rubbish to eat. You never know what you're getting.'

'I'm going back to bed,' Annabel groaned. She couldn't face another minute listening to her mother complaining.

★　★　★

The following day Annabel forced herself to get ready for work.

'You look terrible,' Maggie informed her, peering at her daughter's pale face. 'Surely you're not going back? Why not take another day off? Keep me company. We could have a nice time. We don't do much together.'

'No, I've got to go in,' Annabel replied. 'I promised Daniel I'd sort out all the special offers.'

'But you're not fit enough. If you stayed here you could have a little rest and then you could sit down and help me sift through my clothes. I've loads I don't wear anymore. Then when you're feeling better, we could take them to the charity shop.'

'No, I'm going to work,' Annabel repeated, marvelling at her mother's insensitivity. Watching Maggie sorting out her old clothes was the last thing she felt like doing. She was heartbroken and all her mother could suggest was going to the charity shop! To be fair though, Maggie didn't know Annabel was heartbroken.

'Can't someone else do your work?' Maggie enquired. 'They had to manage when you had your accident.'

'That's the point. They were so good to me I don't want them to think I'm taking liberties. Anyway, I'll be all right.'

Annabel went upstairs to put on some make-up. She studied her appearance in the mirror. Her mother was right, she did look terrible. Her eyes were still puffy from crying and her face was blotchy. She applied the make-up as best she could to hide the ravages of the previous day and night, finished getting ready and crept out of the house without saying goodbye.

When she arrived at the supermarket the first person she saw was Brenda, who peered at her and exclaimed, 'Hello, you don't look very well. Are you sure you should be at work?'

'I'm fine,' Annabel lied. 'I just had a late night.'

'Oh, I see.'

What did Brenda see? Annabel wondered. She could have no conception of the trauma she'd been put through. Brenda probably thought Annabel just had a hangover from drinking too much.

That day seemed endless. Annabel tried to concentrate on her work, but she couldn't get Garry out of her mind. Why had he treated her like that? she asked herself. Why had he deceived her? Surely he must have realised that she would find out in the end. She could never forgive him for what he'd done.

There were more customers in the store than usual and some complained about having to wait in long queues. Annabel found it hard to keep calm and be her normal efficient self.

When Daniel came and asked her how she was getting on sorting out their special offers, she snapped, 'I haven't had time to do them yet. I've been so busy on the till.'

'Okay,' he replied. 'Sorry. I should have realised. Don't worry. Just do them when you can. I know I can trust you.'

'I'll make sure they're done before I leave tonight,' Annabel assured him, feeling guilty for appearing rude. She should be more in control of her feelings. She knew Daniel appreciated what she did. He'd made that quite clear. He was always polite and charming to her, as he was to everyone.

When she arrived home from work that night there were several carrier bags full of clothes piled up in the hall. Annabel found her mother slumped in a chair in the lounge.

'Oh, you're here at last,' Maggie sighed. 'Thank goodness for that. Thought you must have been working late again. You put in too many hours at that supermarket.'

'We need the money. You know that,' Annabel replied through clenched teeth.

'Yes, but I'm sure you spend more time there than anyone else.'

'As I've said before, I am the supervisor. I have a lot of responsibility. Anyway, what's all that stuff piled up in the hall?'

'I've been really busy sorting out my things. Can you take the bags to the charity shop for me another day please, Annabel? It took me ages doing that. I'm worn out.'

I'm worn out too, Annabel thought. *I've had a hard day at work, but she doesn't care. All she thinks about is herself.* 'Okay, I'll go to the charity shop when I get time,' she replied. There was no point in starting an argument with her mother. She was much too tired.

'What are we having for dinner tonight?'

Maggie enquired. I'm starving.'

'So am I. I'll get something in a minute.'

Later, while tossing and turning in bed trying to sleep, Annabel pondered about the flat. Now she had finished with Garry, she didn't know what to do. Should she go ahead with the move or stay with her mother? Eventually she decided it was time to leave home. She would do it. The hard part would be telling Maggie, especially now she wouldn't get moral support from Garry if her mother proved difficult. Gradually Annabel formulated a plan.

★　★　★

One evening a few days later, Annabel cooked her mother's favourite meal.

'That was delicious,' Maggie remarked, putting down her knife and fork. 'I don't know what I'd do without you. I'd never cope. It's a good thing you haven't moved away, dear.' She patted her daughter's hand.

This was not going to plan, Annabel thought. After that statement, how could she tell her mother she was going to move?

'You're better off without your . . . your policeman, or any man, come to that. Just you and me together, that's the best thing,' Maggie continued.

Annabel pulled her hand away and took a deep breath. It was now or never, she told herself. 'Mother,' she exclaimed, 'You'd manage very well on your own. You're not old or . . . or ill. You don't need me to look after you, and . . . and . . . '

'And? Stop stammering, Annabel. What are you trying to say?'

'I'm moving into a flat of my own next week.'

'You're what?' Maggie gasped.

'I've put a deposit on a flat and I'm moving in next week,' Annabel repeated more boldly.

'Oh no!' Maggie shrieked. 'It's that Garry. He's put you up to this. I suppose you've made it up with him and you're moving in together. I knew he was up to no good, enticing you away from me.'

'It's nothing to do with Garry . . . ' Annabel started to explain. 'I decided . . . '

She stopped when Maggie let out a piercing wail. 'You decided! Oh, you ungrateful girl!' She banged her fist down on the table. 'After all I've done for you. How can you treat me like this? I don't deserve it. I'm so unlucky!'

'Don't get upset, Mother.' Annabel spoke calmly as if to a young child.

'Upset! I'm heartbroken. First of all, your father died. Now you're leaving me. What have I ever done wrong?'

'You've done nothing wrong.' That wasn't strictly true, Annabel thought. Hadn't Maggie bullied her for years and made constant demands upon her? However, now was not the time to bring all that up. Other tactics were needed. 'I'm not going far away,' Annabel added. 'I'll still be able to see you frequently.'

'It's a wonder you're not putting me in a care home. You wouldn't have to worry about me at all then,' Maggie sobbed.

'Don't tempt me,' Annabel muttered under her breath, but aloud she said, 'Don't be so ridiculous, Mother. Why would I do that?'

'To get rid of me, of course.'

'This is ludicrous!' Annabel shouted. 'I'm just trying to make you see sense. Care homes are for the elderly and infirm. You are fit and well and quite capable of looking after yourself.'

'I'm not. My arthritis is very bad.'

'It might not be so bad if you made more effort to do things for yourself! It wouldn't hurt you to do more around the house,' Annabel exploded. 'Exercise is what you need. You're lazy, that's what you are!'

'How can you say that when I'm in constant pain? Stop bullying me.'

'Now you know what I've had to put up with for years.'

'That's a lie. I've never bullied you,' Maggie sobbed.

'Okay. Let's change the subject,

please,' Annabel said more quietly. She could see she was going to get nowhere with her mother that night.

'Where are you moving to then?' Maggie sniffed.

'Just around the corner, Lennox Gardens. It's nice there. You can come and visit me whenever you like.' Annabel tried hard to placate her mother.

'I won't come if that Garry's there. It's not right living with someone you're not married to. They didn't do it in my day. We knew how to behave. What's the world coming to, I'd like to know? Men and women living together without being married. Disgusting! That's what I call it.' Maggie was in full flow now. 'You . . . '

'I'm not living with Garry,' Annabel interrupted. She didn't want to hear any more.

'You're not?' Maggie's eyes widened. 'Then why do you want to move? I suppose it's so I can't see what you and Garry are getting up to.'

That had been the intention originally, Annabel thought, but now it no longer applied. She wouldn't be seeing Garry again. 'It's time I had my own home, Mother. I can't live with you forever.'

'Why not?'

'I'm grown up. I've got to become independent some time, and now seems the right moment.'

'How will I manage without you?'

'Very well. As I've said before, you're not an invalid or old. You are perfectly capable of looking after yourself. Besides, I won't be far away if you need me.'

'It's that Garry who's influenced you. I know it is. You never had those ideas before he came along.'

'It's nothing to do with Garry. I should have moved out years ago.'

'I suppose the next thing will be, he'll entice you off to Australia or some other country thousands of miles away. I'll never see you again. Oh, what am I going to do?' Maggie sobbed noisily.

The way my mother's carrying on, emigrating sounds very tempting, Annabel thought, but she replied, 'Stop upsetting yourself. I'm not going to Australia or any other country. I'll be just around the corner.'

'You might say that now, but Garry won't be content until he's got you where he wants you. He'll take you away from me.'

That was what she would have liked, Annabel mused — to get away from all this complaining and whining. She wouldn't be doing it with Garry, but at least having her own flat would give her some reprieve from her mother. She answered, 'Stop blaming Garry. This is nothing to do with him. It's my decision. I've told you, it's time I had my own home and . . . and . . . '

'And what?' Maggie interrupted.

'I . . . I told you, I'm finished with Garry.'

'You are?' A smile broke out on Maggie's face. 'You haven't made it up with him?'

'No.'

'I told you no good would come from it,' Maggie gloated. 'I knew right from the start it would all end in disaster.'

How right she was! Maybe she should have listened to her mother then, Annabel thought grudgingly as she replied, 'Now I've told you, let's talk about something else.'

'What did Garry do?' Maggie didn't want to change the subject. She wanted to hear all the details.

'It's none of your business,' Annabel snapped.

'Don't shout at me just because Garry's treated you badly. You don't have to do the same to me.'

'I'm not shouting.' Annabel tried to speak calmly, thinking, *But you don't care how badly you treat me*. 'When I'm settled in my new home,' she continued, 'You can come over to dinner and I'll pop in to see you from time to time. It'll be good for you. Give you a chance to make new friends.'

'How will I do that?'

'Join a club or something.'

'I don't like clubs.'

'You've never been to any. How do you know you don't like them until you've tried them?'

'They're full of old people hobbling around on zimmer frames talking about the good old days. That's not for me.'

Annabel had to laugh. 'It depends on what sort you go to. There are clubs for all age groups, or you could join an evening class and learn something new — maybe a foreign language — or take up photography, or painting.'

'I'm no good at those kinds of things. Besides, I won't go out at night.'

'Well, go to a daytime class then. There are plenty of different subjects you could study. I'm sure you'd find something you liked, if you tried.' *Mum's so negative*, Annabel was thinking, *putting obstacles in the way of everything I suggest.*

'I doubt it. Anyway, I'm not interested.'

'Well, I can't help you then. You'll

have to sort yourself out.'

Maggie caught hold of Annabel's arm. 'Tell me why you finished with Garry. That's what I'd like to know.'

'I don't want to talk about it.'

'I suppose you found out he was married.'

Annabel had heard enough. She wasn't going to prolong this conversation. She grabbed a jacket off a hook and hurried to the front door, calling over her shoulder, 'I'm going out. I need some fresh air.'

'Come back!' Maggie yelled.

Annabel ignored her cries and marched out of the house. She wandered about the streets hardly knowing what she was doing or where she was going, as had happened many times since the day of the party. How could Garry have been so cruel? she kept thinking. How could he have hoped to get away with what he had done?

Annabel became aware that her mobile phone was ringing. It was Garry yet again. She switched it off. She wouldn't give him the satisfaction of getting an answer. She'd never forgive him. She'd thought he was decent and honest but he wasn't. He'd deceived her in the worst possible way. Were all men like that? she wondered. No, her father hadn't been. He'd been true to her mother until the day he died. He'd doted on her, spoilt her completely. That was why she was finding it so hard to cope now. *But she'll have to cope soon though, when I move out,* Annabel mused. *She'll have no choice.*

For weeks Annabel had dreamt of what it would be like living in her own flat, with Garry visiting her frequently. But now those dreams were shattered forever. She'd placed her trust in him and he'd betrayed her.

Annabel's mind went back to the day of the party. It had started so well. She'd realised then that she'd fallen in love with Garry and had hoped he felt the same way. When he'd arrived at the door to collect her he'd said that she looked wonderful. Other people had also complimented her on the new turquoise silk dress and she'd felt elegant and sophisticated. This was something she was not used to. Previously, on the few occasions when she'd been invited to a party or other celebration, she'd felt invisible amongst all the attractive women who'd been there. But now since meeting Garry she'd managed to lose quite a few pounds in weight and had promised herself she'd never put them back on. She'd also learned to dress more fashionably and was sporting a new modern hairstyle.

That night, before Garry had arrived at Annabel's home to collect her, she'd taken a lot of care with her appearance. When she looked in the mirror she hardly recognised herself. Plain Annabel had turned into a swan. Her eyes were sparkling, her hair was gleaming and for once it had gone just right. She felt like Cinderella going to the ball.

Garry also was looking incredibly handsome that night. He was very attentive towards Annabel and she'd never felt so happy. They were sitting together holding hands, trying to get their breath back after participating in a very lively dance when, bending close to her, Garry whispered, 'You have very beautiful eyes, my Belle.'

Annabel flushed with pleasure. She was glad that she'd worn her new eye shadow and mascara. No one had ever noticed her eyes before. 'Thank y . . . ' she started to say when she was interrupted by someone coming over, slapping Garry on the back and saying, 'Hello.'

That was when the party was ruined.

'Haven't seen you around for ages,' the stranger continued. 'Glad you made it, Garry. I know how elusive you policemen can be.' Then he turned to Annabel, took hold of her hand, shook it and said, 'So pleased to meet you at last. It's Chloe, isn't it?'

Annabelle looked at him in surprise, which quickly turned to horror as he went on. 'Garry, where have you been hiding your gorgeous wife all this time?'

7

A long silence ensued, which to Annabel seemed like an eternity. She snatched her hand away from the stranger and stared at Garry, willing him to give some plausible explanation, but none was forthcoming. He, too, looked in total shock. All the while his friend was gazing from one to the other, waiting for an answer.

Then Garry regained his composure, took a deep breath and answered, 'No, this . . . this is Annabel, my . . . my girlfriend.'

'But . . . but I . . . I thought . . . ' His friend started to reply, then tailed off. Seeing Annabel's horror-struck face, he realised he'd made a dreadful mistake. 'I'm sorry, I didn't know — '

'Chloe and I have separated,' Garry quietly interrupted his friend, who looked mortified.

'I must apologise,' he murmured. 'I . . . I . . . wish I'd kept quiet. I'd no idea. If you'll excuse me, I think I'll get myself a drink.' He hurried away, still muttering to himself.

Garry was looking intently at Annabel, who appeared too stunned to say anything. Then he turned to her and said, 'I . . . I'm so sorry you had to find out this way.'

'Oh,' she gasped, suddenly finding her voice, 'Chloe, your . . . your wife? You . . . you . . . ' She stopped, unable to carry on, as she choked back an almighty sob. She was aware of a group of people nearby. She felt they were all staring at them, watching the spectacle. Annabel clutched her handbag tightly and fled to the ladies' cloakroom, her eyes so full of tears that she could hardly see where she was going.

'Wait, Annabel,' she heard Garry calling after her. 'I can explain everything.'

She ignored him. Her one thought was to get away as fast as she could.

She pulled open the cloakroom door, saw that it was empty and collapsed onto a sofa which was placed in front of a long mirror. She sobbed uncontrollably for several minutes, seemingly unaware of where she was or what she was doing. *Garry's married and he never told me* was echoing round and round in her head. Gradually her tears subsided and anger took over. *How could he do this to me?* she thought. *Why didn't he tell me?*

Several minutes later, the door was opened and a young woman came in. 'Are you all right?' she enquired tentatively.

Annabel recognised her from earlier on as one of Garry's work colleagues. Suddenly her anger was turned to embarrassment. All Garry's friends had been witness to the horrible scene. They probably knew that he was married. She was the stupid one being taken in by him, thinking that he was single like herself. She should have been less trusting. *I've got to get out of here,* she thought. Annabel became aware that the young woman was still standing in front of her, waiting for an answer, so she made a great effort to pull herself together. 'No, I'm not all right,' she snapped. 'I'm going home.'

'Oh, don't do that. Not yet. Garry wants to see you.'

'Well, I don't want to see him.'

'He's very upset,' the young woman said.

'He's upset!' Annabel shrieked. 'What does he think I am?'

'Just come in and talk to him,' she urged. 'He wants to explain everything to you.'

'I don't want to hear. I've finished with him.'

'But I think you've got the wrong idea.'

'No, I haven't. How can I have the wrong idea? Garry's married and he didn't tell me. I understand it all now.'

'Give him a chance.'

'After what he's done? Not likely!'

'But if you heard what he has to say,

you might change your mind.'

'Never,' Annabel replied defiantly. 'Anyway, why are you so concerned about Garry?' She looked suspiciously at the young woman. 'Can't he speak for himself? Why has he sent you in here to do his dirty work for him?'

'He can't come in the ladies' cloakroom, can he?' the young woman replied. 'So he sent me to have a word with you; thought I might be able to make you see sense.'

'Oh the cheek! The arrogance of the man! Who does he think he is?' Annabel was beside herself with rage.

'I know you've had a bit of a shock, but if you calm down and listen to what he has to say, I think you might understand.'

'I won't!'

'Please come back with me.' The young woman tried to take hold of Annabel's arm but she shrugged her off.

'I don't know what motive you have for defending Garry, but you can tell him I want nothing more to do with him.'

'Look Annabel, I work with Garry at the station. I've been with him for a few years. He's a decent chap. I know he wouldn't deliberately do anything to hurt anyone.'

'I'm not interested in any of your excuses. As far as I'm concerned, I don't ever want to see Garry again, and you can tell him that. We're finished. I'm leaving.' Annabel pushed open the cloakroom door, slunk over to the main entrance of the hall and ran outside, ignoring the curious glances which were directed at her. She could see Garry advancing towards her, but slammed the door in his face.

'Anna,' he called as he caught up with her. 'Please wait.' He pushed the door away and grabbed hold of her arm. Her handbag fell to the ground and some of the contents spilled out onto the floor. 'Just let me talk to you.'

'Let go of me!' Annabel shrieked. 'Now look what's happened.'

'I'm sorry,' Garry murmured quickly, gathering up some of the articles.

She yanked her arm away, snatched the objects from him, picked up the rest and yelled, 'Leave me alone!'

'Please listen, Anna. I can explain everything.' His voice was low and pleading. She flinched as he took hold of her hand once more.

'There's nothing to explain,' she said bitterly. 'You have a wife, which you omitted to tell me. What else is there to say?' Annabel forced her arm from his grip. She clutched her bag tightly. 'I want to go home.'

'Chloe, my . . . wife and I are separated. We're going to get a divorce.'

Annabel stood facing Garry, her body rigid in anger. 'A likely story. That . . . that's what men always say when . . . when they're caught out. I'm not listening to any more.'

'It'll be soon, Anna. Please hear me out. I'll be divorced in a few weeks and then I'll be free.'

'So you say. More lies . . . '

'It's true. I wouldn't lie about something like that.'

'Wouldn't you?'

'Of course not. Please calm down and give me a chance to explain.'

'It's too late for explanations. I don't want to hear.' Annabel choked back a sob. 'We're finished. I never want to see you again.' She looked around and spotting a taxi parked nearby, ran over, got inside and was whisked away while Garry stood watching, a look of desperation on his face.

★ ★ ★

A few days after Annabel had told her mother she was moving into her own flat, she decided to start sorting some of her possessions which were on shelves in the lounge. She made two piles. One was for the objects she wanted to keep and the other was to be taken to a charity shop. Maggie was hovering in the background, moaning and complaining. 'Don't do it, Annabel. Stay

121

here with me. I need you.'

'You don't need me. You're perfectly capable of looking after yourself.'

'I'm not. You're so cruel. Always thinking about yourself.'

'And you don't?' Annabel yelled, her patience beginning to fail.

'How dare you say that to me? I'm your mother.' Maggie stamped her foot.

'How could I ever forget?' Annabel muttered under her breath.

'What did you say?' Maggie asked. 'Speak up.'

'Nothing.'

'I suppose it was something nasty. I don't understand you anymore.'

'You never did.'

'Pardon?'

'I'm busy!' Annabel shouted. 'Can you hear that?'

'You don't have to shout. I'm not deaf.'

'No, only when you want to be.'

'You're so unkind, Annabel. What did I do to deserve a daughter like you?' Maggie groaned. She sat down and put her head in her hands. 'Oh, what's going to become of me?'

Annabel had heard enough. 'I can't stand here all day arguing with you,' she answered. 'I've things to do upstairs. I'll see you in the morning.' She hurried out of the lounge and climbed the stairs, ignoring the remarks which her mother hurled after her. She went into her bedroom, locked the door, took a couple of suitcases out of the wardrobe and started throwing garments inside.

Suddenly Annabel caught sight of the beautiful turquoise silk dress she'd worn for the party that terrible night. She wanted to shred it to pieces. She'd been so happy when she'd put it on. She'd felt young and attractive. She'd been ready for a new phase in her life, until those few simple words uttered by Garry's friend had shattered all her dreams. Now she was back to being plain Annabel Barker and probably always would be. She'd never wear that dress again. Why should she keep it? It would remind her of what Garry had done. She pulled it out of the wardrobe and flung it onto her bed.

She'd feel better if she destroyed it. Annabel looked on the dressing table for her scissors, but they were not there. Then she remembered that she'd left them in the top drawer. She'd put them there the other day when she'd been tidying her bedroom. She opened the drawer, grabbed hold of them and was just about to cut the dress into shreds when something stopped her. In her head she could hear the words, 'It's too good to destroy.'

It was as if she'd heard her father's voice. He'd always been a thrifty person. 'Waste not, want not,' he'd often said.

That was the motto he'd lived by. He'd have been horrified if he'd seen her desecrating something so beautiful in such a wanton fashion.

No, she couldn't ruin that dress. She'd take it to the charity shop, along with all the other items she no longer needed. Someone else would be glad to have it, even though she had no further use for it. Annabel hung it back in the wardrobe.

Then she spotted the matching handbag which was lying on the floor at the back. She'd been so pleased when she'd discovered it in her local group of shops, and had been even more delighted when the shop assistant told her the price had been reduced by half. It was the exact colour of her dress. She'd carried the bag with pride that night. Several guests had complimented her on it. With trembling fingers, Annabel opened it. Inside was the new lipstick and bottle of scent she'd purchased for the party. The smell of the perfume wafted from the bag and memories of that dreadful evening came flooding back. She hurled the bag back into the wardrobe and fell onto the bed, sobbing. She'd remember that night until her dying day.

For the next few days Annabel continued to be busy sorting her possessions ready for the move. She discovered that she had a lot of clothes which were now too big for her. She placed these in bags ready to take to the charity shop on her day off. She would never wear those again, she mused. She had no intention of re-gaining all the weight she'd lost in the past weeks. She would be very careful with her diet. At first she'd lost weight intentionally to look trim for the fateful party, but since that night her appetite had dwindled and she'd eaten less than usual, so consequently she looked and felt a great deal slimmer.

Even her mother had noticed. 'You look terrible,' she said one day. 'It doesn't suit you, being so skinny.'

'I'm far from skinny,' Annabel retorted, 'but I do want to get slimmer.'

'A girl looks better with a bit of flesh on her. That's what I think. You're getting quite scrawny. You used to be nice and round.'

'That was the trouble. I needed to lose weight, but I was too lazy to do anything about it, so now I've started dieting, I'm not going to give it up.'

'It was that Garry who put all this

nonsense into your head. You're better off without him,' Maggie replied.

'I'm not going to argue with you,' Annabel answered. She didn't want to talk about Garry with her mother. 'I need to finish sorting out my things.' She tried to walk away, but Maggie grabbed her arm.

'You're not really going ahead with the move, are you? There's no need now Garry's off the scene.'

'Look, I've told you before. It's all settled; I'm moving on Saturday. I don't want to discuss it anymore, so please leave me in peace.' Annabel gently pushed her mother aside and hurried upstairs. She locked her bedroom door, switched on some music and started throwing things into boxes.

While Annabel was packing, she caught sight once more of the turquoise dress and the matching handbag, which was still lying at the bottom of the wardrobe where she had thrown it in a fit of despair. She picked them up and put them with the items that were to be taken away. 'I definitely don't need those anymore,' she said aloud. Suddenly she realised that she'd calmed down a lot in the past few days. Now she could look at that dress without bursting into tears. She'd learnt a lesson from Garry. She'd be less trusting in the future, and if any other man should show interest in her she'd be much more wary and cautious.

* * *

The move went very smoothly. The only problem Annabel had was with her mother. When it was time to leave Maggie stood in the doorway sobbing and moaning dramatically. 'What am I going to do?' She kept on repeating.

'You'll manage quite well,' Annabel tried to reassure her. 'I've left your tea in the fridge and there's plenty of food for tomorrow. There's salad, fresh vegetables and a loaf of bread too. The freezer's full up, so you won't need to go shopping for a few days unless you want to.'

'You're so cruel, Annabel,' Maggie whimpered. 'You really shouldn't be doing this. I'm getting old. It's all too much for me. All this worry could give me a heart attack. I could drop down dead in front of you, just like your . . . your father did. How would you feel then?'

'That's not fair, Mum, bringing that up.' Annabel fought back the tears. She'd never got over the shock of being with her father when he'd passed away. This was not the time to be thinking of that. 'Anyway, you're not old and there's nothing wrong with your heart. You're not even sixty yet. Stop trying to give me a guilty conscience. It's no good you carrying on like this. I'm moving and that's that.'

'Wilful, that's what you are!' Maggie shouted.

Finally everything was packed into the removal van. Annabel kissed her mother and said, 'You can come over for dinner one evening next week. I'll ring you up to arrange it.'

Maggie ignored her daughter and stomped off into the house, slamming the front door.

She even has to spoil my moving day, Annabel thought. *Because she's unhappy, she begrudges me any chance of happiness. Maybe in a day or two when she's got used to the situation, she'll come round and act more reasonably. I'll have to try and forget about her tantrums. I won't let her ruin my life too. I've been hurt enough by Garry. Now I'm going to start a fresh chapter in my life.*

8

Annabel was busy for the next couple of days settling into her flat, and had little time to dwell on her failed relationship with Garry. At night she was so tired she fell into an exhausted sleep.

Daniel had given her two days off work, for which she was very grateful. She scrubbed and polished everywhere and the flat looked neat and clean. She felt quite proud of her achievement. It was her first attempt at homemaking and she thought she'd made a good job of it. She thoroughly enjoyed arranging her possessions and stood back to admire her handiwork. Even her mother should be impressed with this, she thought. She hoped that after a few days her mum would get used to being on her own and would be more reasonable.

Annabel telephoned her in the evening, but she said very little apart from complaining that she was very lonely. 'Try to go out and make friends,' Annabel advised. 'There's a women's meeting at the church. Why don't you go along and see what it's like?'

'I don't go to church,' Maggie replied.

'That doesn't matter. I'm sure you could still go to it.'

'Don't fancy it.'

'What about the college then? They have all sorts of classes there. You might find one on needlework or tapestry. You used to enjoy doing embroidery when I was young. You were always making chair backs and cushion covers.'

'I didn't have arthritis then,' Maggie moaned.

'Well, I'm sure there's something you could do. Anyway, would you like to come round on Wednesday evening?'

'I don't know.'

'I'll come and collect you after work. It's not too far.'

'My legs might be bad.'

'I'm sure you'll be able to walk to my flat.' Annabel was trying to be patient.

My Mum's impossible, she was thinking. *She's so negative about everything. Thank goodness I've had the sense to move out. I should have done this years ago. At least I won't have to put up with her grumbling too often.*

'I can't go fast,' Maggie added.

'That's okay.'

'What are we going to eat?'

'I'll make a shepherd's pie,' Annabel promised, knowing it was her mother's favourite meal.

'Good. All right, I'll come then.'

You're not doing me any favours, so don't be so condescending, Annabel felt like saying, but instead decided it was wisest to say nothing. She didn't want to start any more rows.

After she'd finished the conversation with her mother, as it was a hot evening Annabel decided to go onto her balcony. She made a mug of coffee, put on her sunglasses, carried a chair outside and sat drinking, surveying the scene around her. She made a mental note to buy herself a couple of garden chairs to put out here. She could see a few other people also enjoying the evening air, some on balconies and others lounging in their gardens. It was very pleasant listening to the birds singing, the bees buzzing and the distant sounds of children playing. So peaceful, she thought, and very different from the past evenings she'd spent with her mother, when they'd had constant arguments. She was very glad that was behind her. Now they had the opportunity of building a new and better relationship. She hoped her mother would realise this too. Annabel decided that after all the hassle of previous months this was what she needed now — a quiet, strife-free life. It didn't sound very exciting, but maybe in a few weeks when she'd rested she'd find herself some new challenges.

Annabel's eyes closed as she thought back over past events and planned what she might do in the future. Perhaps she would join a club or attend an evening class herself and make some friends, as she had advised her mother to do. This was what she lacked — a close friend, someone in whom she could confide. She'd never found it easy to make friends as other girls did. She'd always been rather shy and diffident, except at the supermarket where as the supervisor she'd felt obliged to exert her authority. Annabel had shown great competence there so Daniel Owen's father had given her the job. She knew that some members of staff thought she was too bossy, but since the accident she'd tried to be less formal and more approachable. Annabel hoped she'd succeeded. Outside of work, however, was a different matter. This was where she most lacked confidence and was inclined to be quite timid.

When she'd met Garry she'd had an instant rapport with him, which was very unusual for her, and her shyness had quickly evaporated. Annabel had been at ease with him from day one, and because of this she'd probably become more relaxed and thus was able to get on better with other people too. So when her relationship with Garry had ended she'd taken it very badly, as she had no one else to turn to. Her mother hadn't helped either, seemingly delighted that Garry was no longer around, so Annabel had felt completely on her own.

Gradually as these thoughts went through her head, she drifted off to sleep wondering what the future would hold. Then suddenly she was startled by the sound of a man's deep voice.

'Hello. I guess you're my new neighbour.'

Annabel jumped, opened her eyes and adjusted her sunglasses, which had fallen over her nose. She looked across the wooden partition to where a tanned young man wearing an open-necked shirt and denim shorts was sitting on a plastic garden bench, drinking a can of beer.

'Hello,' she replied sleepily, stifling a yawn, feeling embarrassed at being caught napping by such a handsome young man.

'Oh, I'm sorry. Did I wake you up?' he apologised. 'I didn't realise you were asleep. I've just come home from work and felt like getting a bit of fresh air. It's been a long day at the office.'

'No, that's quite all right,' Annabel replied shyly. 'I . . . I wasn't really asleep, only dozing. It's so hot. That's why I came outside. At least there's a breeze here. It's unbearable indoors,' she babbled.

'Yes, it is a warm evening. You need to get yourself an electric fan. My name's Jack, by the way.'

'You . . . you're right. I could do with a fan. I'll definitely get myself one. I . . . I'm Annabel but all my friends call me Anna,' she replied hesitantly, wondering if she should tell him this. Would he think she was being a bit too friendly and forward? She was feeling quite unnerved by his presence.

'That's a pretty name. I don't think I have ever met an Annabel before. How are you settling in, Anna?'

'Very well, thank you.' She blushed,

looked away and sipped her coffee, which had gone cold. Suddenly she felt like an immature schoolgirl again. *Pull yourself together*, she told herself. *You're a woman, not a child.*

'These are nice flats, aren't they?' Jack continued, seemingly unaware of her unease.

'They're . . . they're lovely. The rooms are a good size and mine was decorated nicely. I'm very pleased with it.'

'Mine was too. Didn't need to do a thing except move my gear in.'

'Have you lived here long?' Annabel enquired, trying hard to make polite conversation. She hadn't expected to have to do this. What her neighbours would be like was something she hadn't thought about, and she'd certainly not anticipated having such an attractive one.

'About eighteen months,' he replied.

Jack was sitting looking at her across the partition and, feeling she had to say something, Annabel added, 'Having a balcony is a bonus, especially in this hot weather.'

'Yes, most flats don't have one, or if they do it's minute,' he answered.

'That's right,' she agreed.

Then Jack burst out laughing, and Annabel gave him a startled look. She hadn't said anything funny, had she? She hadn't meant to.

'We sound like a couple of estate agents trying to sell these flats,' he chuckled.

'Oh, I see what you mean.' Annabel smiled too.

Jack took a swig of his beer and enquired, 'Are you living here on your own?'

'Yes. What . . . what about you?'

'I'm on my own too . . . now.'

Annabel wondered what that meant but thought it best not to ask. She felt shy and awkward again.

Jack gulped down the rest of his beer. 'That's better,' he said. 'I needed that.'

Annabel picked up her cup of cold coffee and quickly finished it.

'Well Anna,' Jack said, 'I think I'll go in and get myself something to eat. It was nice meeting you. If this hot weather keeps up, I'll probably see you out here again soon. Don't forget, if you need any help just let me know. I'm quite good with flat packs.' He smiled and brushed his rather long, wavy blond hair from his eyes as a gust of wind blew across the balcony. He stood up and Annabel observed that he was over six feet tall and quite muscular. *I guess he spends a fair bit of time at the gym*, she thought.

'Er . . . thanks, Jack. Good night.'

'Good night, Anna. See you soon,' he called as he walked in through the double glass doors.

Annabel sat watching him walk inside.

* * *

The next day she returned to work.

'How did your move go?' Daniel enquired. 'Is there anything I can do to help?'

'That's very kind of you,' Annabel

answered, 'but I don't need any help, thank you. Everything went very smoothly.'

She was thinking, *How many bosses would ask their employees if they needed help moving and actually mean it?* She knew that if it was necessary, Daniel would have given her any assistance he could.

'The previous occupant left the flat in quite good order. There are shelves, cupboards and picture hooks everywhere. I just had to give it a good clean and put away my possessions. I've been really lucky.'

'Good. I hope you'll be very happy there. How does your mother feel about it?'

'I'm afraid she's taken it badly.'

'I'm sorry. I suppose she's finding it hard being on her own.'

'Yes, she is. But she's not old; I'm sure she could make something of her life if she tried.'

'She'll get used to it.'

'I do hope so.'

'Good luck with her.'

'Thanks. I'll need it.'

Daniel smiled and Annabel remembered how she'd felt only a short time ago. She'd had such a crush on him. It embarrassed her now to think about how she'd been unable to take her eyes off him. Her only consolation was that he was so grief-stricken for his wife, he probably hadn't even noticed Annabel.

That was all before Garry came on the scene, she reflected. Now she realised her feelings for Daniel could not have led to anything. He would never have been interested in her. She was much too ordinary for him; not pretty or vivacious enough, like the young woman she had seen him with at the concert. She'd been really glamorous. Annabel wondered if he was still seeing her and whether a relationship was developing between the two. She couldn't help feeling a little jealous of the woman, especially now Annabel seemed destined to be on her own. However, she felt guilty for doing this. *Daniel's had a hard time in the last few years, so he deserves some happiness now*, she told herself. *I shouldn't begrudge him that just because my love life's gone so wrong.*

After work that night, Annabel was leaving the supermarket when she spotted a familiar car outside. She quickly turned round to run back inside, but she was too late. She felt a hand on her arm and a voice said, 'Please Anna, don't run away from me. I need to talk to you. There's so much I have to tell you.'

Annabel tried to pull away but she couldn't. She was held firm. It was the first time she had seen Garry since the night of the party.

9

Annabel was very shocked when Garry met her outside the supermarket. She'd been trying to convince herself that she no longer cared for him and that he wasn't worth bothering about, but when she saw his face, her heart immediately began to beat rapidly and all those hidden feelings came to the surface again. She attempted to get away but it was impossible; he held onto her too tightly.

'Let me go!' she yelled.

'Please Anna, I need to talk to you.'

'There's nothing to talk about. And I'm Annabel, not Anna.'

'Sorry, Anna . . . er, Annabel. There's a lot to talk about. If only you'd listen to me, I could make you understand.'

'Make me?' she exploded. You can't make me do anything.'

'I didn't mean it like that. I just meant that if you gave me the chance to explain, you would understand why I acted as I did. Please, Annabel.'

She wanted to punish him for all the grief he'd given her, but hearing him pleading with her and seeing his pale, sad face and the dark circles under his eyes, part of her wanted to fold him into her arms and say she would forgive him anything. But then the thought came back to her: Garry was married. How could they get around that fact?

'There's no point. Nothing you can say will make any difference.'

'But it can. Please hear me out. Look, why don't we go and have a coffee? It'll give me the opportunity to explain everything, and then you can decide what you want to do. I promise I won't pressurise you. What do you say?'

Annabel hesitated. She was in a quandary. What should she do? She glanced at Garry's face again and found herself weakening. 'Well, just for . . . for . . . a few minutes then.'

He looked so pathetic, standing there. He seemed somehow smaller than she remembered, and much thinner, as if he'd lost a lot of weight.

'But what there is to say, I can't imagine,' she added. 'You neglected to tell me you had a wife. How can you get around that?'

Garry ignored her question and kept hold of her arm as they crossed the road.

'I can walk on my own,' Annabel snapped. 'I'm not going to run away. I've said I'll listen and I will.'

'Thanks, Annabel. You won't regret this.'

That's what he thinks. I'm regretting it already. Why did I let him persuade me? Annabel wondered.

Garry let go of her arm and she stomped along beside him, looking down at the ground. Neither said a word as they made their way to the coffee bar. *Should I be doing this?* Annabel was asking herself. After what he'd done, did he deserve to have a chance to explain himself? She could have refused to go with him, and probably should have, but part of her wanted to know what he had to say. Why was she so weak-willed as far as Garry was concerned? she mused.

He led her to a seat in the corner by the window away from most of the other customers, and went up to the counter to order their drinks. Annabel looked around her. Garry had his back to her. She could run out of here, she was thinking. That would serve him right for what he'd done to her. But something kept her glued to the seat. She guessed it was her insatiable curiosity; she wanted to know what explanation he was going to give her.

A few minutes later he returned, placed their coffees on the table and sat down opposite her. Nobody said a word. Garry was staring at the table as if trying to decide what to say, and she sat watching him.

Finally Annabel barked, 'Well, what have you got to say for yourself? It had better be good.' She knew she sounded like a schoolteacher dealing with a naughty pupil, but she couldn't help it.

She was feeling all the pain and anguish of the past few weeks and she wanted to hurt him back; make him pay for what he'd done.

'I know you're angry with me, Annabel, but . . . but I can explain everything.' He spoke quietly, still looking down at the table as if afraid to catch her eye.

'Can you? I doubt it.' Her feelings of scepticism wouldn't be quelled.

'I'm sorry, Annabel, that I didn't tell you about . . . about . . . '

'Your wife!' she interrupted. 'You didn't tell me you were married. Why not?'

'I . . . I know I should have. But if I had, I thought you wouldn't have gone out with me.'

'No. I wouldn't.'

'You see, that was why I didn't tell you.'

'So you pretended to be single and thought that was all right?' Annabel's voice was full of contempt.

'No, it wasn't like that. I didn't

pretend anything. Just let me explain.'
Garry put his head in his hands.

Annabel was too het up to listen. She had to go on. 'You were living a lie.'

'No.' He raised his head wearily. 'I didn't tell you about Chloe because — '

'You were a dishonest cheat,' Annabel interrupted, her eyes blazing, anger showing in every muscle of her body. She stood up.' I shouldn't have come here with you. It's pointless. Nothing you can say will make any difference.' She hurled the words at him; all her self-control had vanished.

'No, don't go.' Garry jumped up and took hold of her hand. 'Please, Annabel, let me talk.'

She glared at him, trying to pull her hand away, but he held it firmly. Once again his touch had a powerful effect on her. She wanted to escape, but felt drawn to him as if by some almost hypnotic force. She gave up the struggle and slumped onto her chair, her outburst over. Garry released her hand and sat back down too.

Annabel could see the pain etched in his face which matched her own. Suddenly she became aware that people were beginning to look at them. Making a scene was abhorrent to her. She had to stay and listen. 'Okay, you win,' she answered.

'Thanks, Annabel. When . . . when I met you, Chloe and I were separated, waiting for our divorce to come through.' He spoke tentatively. 'So I reasoned that . . . I . . . I was as good as single.'

'You were going to get a divorce? Really?' She looked at him anxiously.

'Yes. I tried to tell you that night of the party.'

He was right. He had tried to tell her, but she was too upset to take it in. She'd refused to listen; her pride had been so badly wounded. She'd believed he was telling lies. 'Go on,' Annabel begged. Now she wanted to hear it all.

'As I said before, I thought that if you knew about Chloe you might not agree to go out with me, and I didn't want to take that risk. I hoped that by the time I'd got round to explaining everything, you and I would be a . . . a couple, so you . . . you wouldn't mind.'

'But that wasn't honest.'

'I know, and I'm truly sorry. I only did it because I liked you and wanted to go out with you, and . . . '

'When you visited me in hospital after the accident you could have told me then,' Annabel interrupted.

'Yes, but as you've already said you wouldn't have gone out with me.'

'No, but if you'd explained properly, I might have.'

'I couldn't take that chance. I didn't want to lose you.'

'You have lost me.'

'Don't say that.'

'It's true though. I don't think I could ever trust you again.'

Garry's face was sorrowful. 'I could try to earn your trust.'

Annabel had mixed feelings. Part of her was glad that he was suffering as she had done, but part of her felt guilty for causing his misery. 'I don't know. How could I be sure that you weren't deceiving me again?'

'I'd never do that. I'm so ashamed of how I treated you.'

'But what about your . . . your wife?'

'Our marriage was all over a long time ago.'

'What happened?'

'I won't go into all the details now, but Chloe and I realised our marriage wasn't working and that we weren't compatible. We did try very hard to make it a success. We even went to see a counsellor but that didn't help, so in the end we could see it was never going to get any better and we decided to separate. Chloe stayed on in our flat and I moved out. After a few months we found we were both much happier apart, so we went to see a solicitor and he suggested we start divorce proceedings.'

'And are you divorced?'

'Not yet, but we will be in a few weeks.'

'So you're not free?'

'I suppose technically I'm not, but in a short time I will be.'

'So when you started going out with me, you weren't really free?' Annabel felt she had to repeat this.

'No, but . . . '

'You were still married to . . . to Chloe?' Annabel interrupted.

'Yes.' Garry's voice was quiet. He looked at her anxiously while she sat silent and motionless, trying to take it all in. After a while he asked, 'So will you forgive me, Annabel?'

'I don't know. I've got to think about all this.' That was true. Her mind was in turmoil. She wanted to forgive, him but after the heartbreak of the past weeks she wasn't sure if she could.

'I can understand that. Look, Annabel, I won't rush you. Take as much time as you need to think things over, and then when you're ready let me know your answer.'

'My answer?'

'Yes. Whether you can ever forgive

me and we can start all over again.'

'Oh, I see.' Did she see? Garry wanted them to get back together as if nothing had happened? Was that it? Could she do that? She really didn't know. She didn't want to experience all that pain again.

'But remember this, Annabel — I never deliberately set out to hurt or deceive you. I wish I'd acted differently and not been so stupid, but there's nothing I can do about it now. It's always easy to be wise after the event. I just hope you realise I'm telling the truth and trying to put things right.'

'Yes, I believe you,' she whispered, 'and I'll think about what you've said.' Annabel picked up her handbag. 'I'd like to go home now, Garry. I think we've done enough talking for today.'

'Okay. I'll take you home.'

'No, it's still light. It's a nice evening and I would rather go on my own.' She needed some fresh air and a walk. Besides, she hadn't told Garry that she'd moved from her mother's house.

She would tell him another time, she thought. Then it dawned on her that she already knew what she was going to do; what reply she would give. She didn't need time to think about it, but she wasn't going to tell Garry that. She'd make him wait for her answer. She wasn't going to make it easy for him.

'All right, if that's what you want,' he replied, looking somewhat crestfallen.

'I do. Thanks for the coffee. Good night, Garry.' She got up from the table.

'Good night, Annabel. You will let me know what you decide?' He was staring at her intently. How long could she resist his pleading little boy look?

'Yes, I'll ring in a few days.'

'I'll be waiting.' Garry watched as she walked out of the coffee bar.

That night Annabel lay in bed re-living the events of the evening. She was so glad she was in her own home and hadn't got to face her mother. What a day it had been! She remembered every moment of it. After a busy shift at the supermarket, the last person she'd expected to see was Garry waiting outside. She'd been so miserable for weeks, but now there was a glimmer of hope that life might start to get better. He seemed genuinely sorry for what he'd done and wanted to get back with her. That was what she wanted too, but since the party she'd been puffed up with self-righteous pride and indignation and hadn't given Garry a chance. She'd ring in a few days and give him her answer, but until then she'd make him wait.

However, before that, she had an ordeal to get through. Her mother would be coming to dinner and would be inspecting her flat. That was something she was not looking forward to.

10

Annabel was in a much happier frame of mind at work after her unexpected meeting with Garry. Not even the prospect of having her mother round for dinner could dampen her spirits. Annabel guessed that for the past few weeks since the day of the party, she'd been less cheerful than usual, and may even have been rather rude to some members of staff when they'd asked her what was wrong. She was embarrassed by the whole episode and didn't want anyone to know what had happened, so she wouldn't talk about it. Most of the staff were too polite to probe so they probably thought she had gone back to her old ways.

Before the accident, and meeting Garry, Annabel had often found it difficult to do her duties as a supervisor and at the same time be a friend to everyone. She'd felt compelled to exert her superiority, worried that if she didn't, they might take advantage. She knew this was caused by a deep sense of inferiority which had been instilled in her by her mother.

However, under Garry's influence Annabel had blossomed and become much more self-confident; that was, until the day of the party when her life had been turned upside-down and all her old insecurities had re-emerged.

Annabel had decided to get her mother's first visit to the flat out of the way before contacting Garry again. She'd had a text message from him saying he was looking forward to hearing from her, but she hadn't replied. She'd do that when her mother had gone home.

Just before she finished work at the supermarket, Daniel Owen had a word with her about re-arranging some of the shelves in order to make a better display of their special offers.

'I'll get onto that first thing in the

morning,' Annabel promised. 'I'm sorry I can't stay behind now, but I've got to go and collect my mother. She's coming round to my flat for supper tonight.'

'Will this be the first time she's seen it?'

'Yes, and I'm not looking forward to it.' Annabel grimaced.

'Well, the best of luck.'

'I'll need it.'

'And don't worry about the shelves; tomorrow will be fine. Have a good evening.' He smiled. 'I'll be thinking of you.'

'Thanks, Daniel.' He was such a good boss, Annabel thought once again. He really cared about his staff. A few months ago she'd have been over the moon if he'd told her he'd be thinking about her, but now she knew that was just the way he was — a very kind person. He'd say the same to any member of staff.

Annabel left work on time and hurried off to collect her mother from home. Maggie held tightly onto her arm as she huffed and puffed her way to the flat. 'It's too far for me to walk,' she grumbled. 'My legs have been really bad today, and it's so hot. Slow down, girl. We're not running a race.'

'Sorry, Mum.' Annabel slackened her pace.

'I hope you've got a fan,' Maggie muttered.

'Yes, I'll put it on as soon as we get in.'

'Good. We'll need it. What are we having for dinner?'

'Your favourite, shepherd's pie.'

'I hope the meat's fresh,' Maggie muttered. 'You didn't buy any of that frozen muck, did you? Don't know what they put in it. The last thing I want is to get a dose of food poisoning.'

'I've been cooking your meals for years and I haven't poisoned you yet, so why are you making such a fuss tonight?' Annabel was trying not to lose her temper. She knew her mother was finding it hard coming to terms with living on her own, so she didn't want to upset her. She'd try the patience of a saint, Annabel was thinking, *and I'm certainly not one of those.*

'Well, you can never be too careful,' Maggie puffed. 'Are we nearly there yet?'

'Not far now,' Annabel reassured her. 'I bought the best minced steak I could find and made it into a shepherd's pie and put it into the freezer. Last night I took it out and left it in the fridge to defrost. So all I've got to do tonight is to cook it in the oven for about three quarters of an hour while I get the vegetables ready. Does that suit you?'

'You don't have to be sarcastic,' Maggie mumbled.

'I wasn't.'

'I hope it will be all right. What would you do if I was suddenly taken ill?'

'I'd phone for an ambulance, of course. What do you think I'd do?'

'Yes, but what if I became ill when I was back at home on my own?'

'You'd have to ring for an ambulance

yourself or ring me, but it's not going to happen.'

'How do you know?'

'I don't,' Annabel snapped, her patience wearing thin.

She was relieved that they were approaching her block of flats. 'Here we are, Mum.' We've arrived.'

'Thank goodness for that,' Maggie mumbled breathlessly. 'I thought we were never going to get there.'

'It didn't take long. Only about fifteen minutes.'

'It seemed longer to me.'

Does she ever stop moaning? Annabel thought. 'Let's take the lift.'

'I hope it's working.'

'Yes, here it comes.' Annabel ushered her mother into the lift, pressed the button, and soon they'd arrived and were walking along the corridor towards her front door. 'Welcome to my home, Mum. You're my first visitor.'

'So I should think. Who else is there to invite? You haven't any friends and your boyfriend's gone. There's no one else to invite, is there?'

Thanks for reminding me I haven't many friends, even if it is true, Annabel thought. *I really wanted to hear that! I'm definitely not going to mention meeting Garry again. I'll wait and see how things go first.*

'Why do you always have to belittle me?' Annabel asked with gritted teeth, inwardly fuming, trying not to say something she would later regret. *Why do I put up with it?* she was asking herself.

'I'm only speaking the truth,' Maggie muttered.

Annabel helped her mother through the door, resisting the urge to leave her standing outside. She led her into the lounge, plumped up the cushions on the sofa and said, 'Come and sit here, Mum.'

Maggie lumbered over and sank down onto the sofa. 'Put the fan on,' she ordered. 'It's too hot in here.'

'Give me a chance.' *She wants her own personal servant,* Annabel was thinking as she plugged the fan in.

'So are you going to invite anyone else here?' Maggie enquired again.

'I might ask one or two of my work colleagues round one evening. They've said they would like to come.'

'What about your boss? Are you going to invite him?'

'I don't know. I haven't thought about it.'

'Now he's someone worth knowing. Such a nice man. You should try and cultivate him as a friend — so much better than that pushy policeman of yours.'

There she goes again, Annabel thought, *criticising Garry. I don't know why she dislikes him so. I dread to think what she would say if she knew I was going to make it up with him. It's a good thing I've moved away from her. At least most of the time I won't have to put up with her complaining, and she won't be able to see what I'm doing.*

'If I asked Daniel, he probably would

come,' Annabel answered, 'but I don't think I will. He's found himself a girlfriend.'

'A girlfriend! Oh Annabel, you've missed your chance there.' Maggie looked horror-struck. 'You silly girl! You've got no idea how to attract a man! When I was your age — well, actually a good few years younger — I had all the young men queuing up, wanting to go out with me. Why did I have such a dull, plain daughter?' she moaned.

'I'm going to put the kettle on,' Annabel stated, forcing herself to keep calm. How could she be so unkind? She didn't think her mum realised she was being offensive.

'What about our supper?' Maggie asked.

'I'll get that started too.'

'Don't take too long. You know I have to eat regularly.'

'I do know that,' Annabel answered sharply.

She fled to the kitchen, thinking, *I can't take much more of this*. She made a cup of tea and was just going to take it in to her mother when her mobile phone sounded. She quickly looked at it and found another message from Garry saying he hoped to hear from her soon. *I'll reply later when my Mum's gone*, she thought.

Maggie tucked into an enormous meal and afterwards Annabel showed her around the flat. She guessed her mother was impressed by it as she didn't make any negative remarks.

'I suppose it's all right,' she said grudgingly, 'but a bit on the small side, and you haven't got much furniture. It's rather bare.'

'It's big enough for me,' Annabel replied. 'I've only just moved in and haven't been able to buy everything I need yet. Do you fancy sitting on the balcony?'

'Yes, I don't mind. It's a lovely evening again.'

Annabel carried two chairs outside and placed some drinks on a little side table. Maggie sat back and took in the view. 'It's not bad round here,' she said. That was praise indeed, Annabel thought. She must like the flat.

A few minutes later the door to the next flat opened and Jack came out onto the balcony. 'Hello, Anna,' he called. 'How's everything?' Then catching sight of her mother, he added, 'Sorry, I didn't realise you had a guest.'

'Hello, Jack. I'm very well, thank you. This is my mother.'

'Pleased to meet you, Mrs . . . er . . . '

'Barker,' Annabel informed him.

'How do you do?' Maggie answered primly. 'I wanted to see Annabel's flat.' She emphasised the word 'Annabel'.

'Do you like it, Mrs Barker?'

'Seems quite nice,' Maggie replied.

'Glad you think so. I'm very pleased with mine. How's work, Anna — er, Annabel?'

She was pleased Jack had taken the hint and used her full name. Maggie hated people calling her Anna. She could never understand why, but supposed it was just another one of her mother's funny quirks.

'Busy,' Annabel answered, 'but I made sure I left on time today.'

'Where do you work?'

'Glentree Supermarket. I'm the supervisor.'

'Oh, that explains it. As soon as I saw you I thought I recognised you. I must have seen you in the store.'

'You probably have. I've been there a long time. What about you, Jack? Where do you work?'

'I commute into London each day. I work in a boring office, doing accounts all day long. Not very exciting I'm afraid, but it pays the bills.'

'I can't say mine's that thrilling either, but the staff are nice and I have a good boss.'

'That's important. Don't you agree, Mrs Barker?'

Annabel was pleased he was trying to bring her mother into the conversation. She'd been sitting listening to the two young people, looking from one to the other but saying nothing.

'Yes, you're right. I keep telling Annabel that,' Maggie replied. 'He's a lovely man. Her boss would make someone a lovely husband.' She stared at Annabel, who blushed and looked away.

Now my mother's embarrassing me, she thought. What must Jack be thinking?

'The poor man's a widower, you know,' Maggie continued. 'Very tragic. It was . . . him losing his wife like that.'

'Oh, I didn't know.'

'Well, it was about three years ago, so I said to my daughter it's time he found himself someone else.'

'And now he has,' Annabel added.

'That's good.' Jack smiled at her. 'Do you work, Mrs Barker?' he asked.

'No, not anymore. Had to give it up. My arthritis is so bad.'

'Oh, I'm sorry to hear that.'

'I had to retire. The pain was so bad, I just couldn't cope with the travelling to work each day,' Maggie continued.

Annabel thought, *She does exaggerate. Her arthritis isn't that bad. She just makes a fuss.*

'You don't look old enough to be retired,' Jack remarked.

'I'm not.' Maggie smiled. 'I took early retirement.'

'I thought so.'

Mum's in her element now, Annabel thought. *She loves being the centre of attention.*

*   *   *

'Well, I suppose I'd better go in and get myself something to eat,' Jack told them. 'Nice to see you again, Annabel, and don't forget to let me know if you need any help. Good night, Mrs Barker.'

'She might need some help when she gets her new furniture. Her flat's a bit bare at the moment,' Maggie told him.

'Oh Mum, I haven't decided what I want yet.' Annabel could feel her face flushing. She glared at her mother. She wished she wouldn't keep meddling in her affairs. She wasn't even living with her mum now, but she was still trying to organise Annabel.

'As I said before, if you want

someone to erect flat packs, I'm your man,' Jack replied. 'And that applies to you too, Mrs Barker.'

'Thank you.' Maggie beamed at him. 'That's useful to know. You're very kind. I might have something for you to do. Good night, Jack.' She turned to her daughter. 'We'll remember that, won't we?'

Annabel raised her eyebrows and looked helplessly at Jack, but he just smiled and said, 'See you soon.' He waved to them and went inside.

'Come on Annabel, I think it's time we went in too. I'll have to go home soon. Got to summon up my energy for that long walk.'

Annabel was furious with her mother. Either she denigrated her, or she was trying to match-make her with someone she wasn't interested in, or she wanted her all to herself. Why did she have to be like this, always interfering in Annabel's life?

'All right, you go inside, Mum. I'll bring the chairs in.' Annabel made a great effort to keep her thoughts to herself. Saying anything to her mother was useless. They'd only end up having another row and she didn't want that.

When they were back inside Maggie said, 'What a charming man! Now he's someone you ought to get to know. So helpful too! Much better than that policeman, Garry. You've lost out on your boss, so don't waste another opportunity. Jack says he does accounts. That's a good job; probably earns a fair salary too. And he's about your age, and so handsome.'

'Would you like another drink before I take you home?' Annabel changed the subject. She didn't want to get into a discussion about Jack. Yes he was good-looking, and he was a charming man and very helpful, but the only man she was interested in now was still Garry. Also, what her mother hadn't considered was that Jack probably had a girlfriend.

Annabel escorted her mother home. She promised to telephone her frequently and said she could come over for dinner again the following week. 'If you learnt how to text, you could contact me whenever you wanted,' Annabel told her, knowing what the answer would be.

'I can't be bothered with all that nonsense,' her mother replied. As Annabel was leaving, Maggie said, 'Don't forget to look out for your neighbour. You might be onto a good thing getting to know him.'

Annabel pretended she hadn't heard and walked away.

When she got back home she decided to ring Garry. The time had come for her to tell him she had forgiven him and would give him another chance. She dialled his mobile, but that was switched off, so she rang his land line. It was answered immediately.

'Hello,' said a woman's voice. 'Can I help you? I'm sorry Garry isn't here at the moment.'

11

Annabel lay on her bed, staring at the ceiling. For the past two hours she'd been trying to sleep but once again it eluded her, and as before it was all due to Garry. What was he playing at? He'd told her he was sorry for what he'd done and begged for her forgiveness, but now he was up to some new trick.

Annabel had taken her mother home after her visit to the flat and then decided to ring Garry to tell him that she'd forgiven him and wanted to continue seeing him, but some woman had answered his phone. 'Hello,' the woman repeated. Can I help you?'

'I . . . er, w . . . wanted to speak to Garry Jonas.' she'd stammered.

'I'm sorry, Garry isn't here at the moment. Can I take a message?'

'Er . . . n — no thank you. I . . . I'll try again another time.' Annabel tried to make her voice sound normal. She didn't want this woman to know she was upset. Who was she, and why was she in Garry's house?

'Are you sure I can't give him a message?'

'No, I'll leave it.'

'Who's calling?' The woman asked. 'I'll let him know you rang.'

'That won't be necessary. Goodbye.' Annabel hung up, her heart pounding and her eyes filled with tears. Just when she thought everything was going to be all right, she had discovered that Garry had got some other woman in his house.

The next morning Annabel arrived at work in a tired, subdued state. She'd spent the night tossing and turning, trying to decide what to do. She'd alternated between tears of despair and anger. Was that woman Garry's wife? He'd said they were getting a divorce, she reminded herself. So it couldn't be, unless that was a lie.

Or did he have some other girlfriend?

Surely after all he'd said to her, he wouldn't deceive her in that way. Or would he? He hadn't told her about his wife, had he? Doubts kept creeping into her mind. What did she really know about Garry? She'd never even been to his house. After the accident everything had moved swiftly and she'd found herself head over heels in love with him, but she should have been more cautious. She supposed it was her lack of experience with men that had made her that way. She was too trusting.

Or could there be a rational explanation for the woman's presence? But if so, why hadn't she explained who she was? *But you didn't ask*, Annabel reminded herself. *Maybe you should have done. Then at least you would have known and could have avoided all this speculation. Why didn't you leave a message? She did ask if you wanted to. You didn't even give her your name. And don't forget, Garry promised he would never deliberately do anything to hurt you again.* Annabel had believed him at the time, so why was she so full of doubts now? These thoughts had gone round and round in her head all night long.

There were a lot of customers in the supermarket that day so Annabel had little time to dwell on her problems, for which she was glad.

'You look tired,' Daniel said to her as she was getting ready to go home after finishing the late shift.

'It's been a busy day,' she replied.

'It certainly has. Er, Annabel, I've been wondering, how did it go with your mother?'

'Not too bad, thanks. She didn't say much but I think she actually likes my flat.'

'That's good. I'll have to come and check it out some time myself — er, if you want me to.'

'Oh yes, you'll be . . . very welcome. Just let me know when you want to come.' What a surprise! Annabel hadn't expected Daniel to suggest that. She thought if her mum knew, she'd be delighted, as she was always trying to pair her with him. Not that it meant anything. He'd probably say the same thing to any other member of staff who moved house.

'I'll hold you to it,' Daniel replied. 'Thanks, Annabel. I hope you sleep well tonight. You deserve it after all your hard work.'

* * *

Once she arrived home, however, Annabel continued to speculate about the woman and ponder what course of action she should take, finally deciding to wait a few days before attempting to ring Garry again. This would give her time to calm down and plan what she was going to say to him. She would see what answers he had for her. At first she'd been too angry to think clearly, but maybe she'd been hasty in condemning Garry, who was possibly unaware that she'd telephoned and spoken to the woman. There could be a quite innocent explanation for the woman's presence. Or was this just wishful thinking? She didn't know but was determined to find out. She looked at her mobile phone and saw another message from Garry asking if she'd forgiven him yet. *I'll make him wait a little longer*, Annabel thought.

She decided to get some fresh air before the sun disappeared behind the clouds. She carried a chair onto the balcony and saw that Jack was there, sitting and reading. He saw her at once and smiled. 'Hi, Anna. I suppose I can call you that?'

'Yes, of course. It's just my mother who objects.'

'So I gathered. She seems to have rather definite opinions about everything.'

'You can say that again,' Annabel laughed. 'My mother thinks she knows everything. I'm sorry about the other night. She does like to embarrass me.'

'Don't worry. My mother's the same. Makes me squirm; tells all her friends how clever I am.'

'Then she's not like my mum,' Annabel replied. 'She continually tells me how stupid I am.'

'That's not nice.'

'No it isn't, but I'm used to it now.'

'She probably doesn't mean it.'

'I think she does. Oh, I'm so glad I moved out. It's such a relief to get away from her constant nagging and complaining. I should have left home years ago.' Annabel thought, *Why am I saying all this? Jack's almost a stranger, but he's so easy to talk to.*

'Is this the first time you've left home then?' he asked.

'Yes, I'm afraid so. What about you?'

'I haven't lived with my parents for years.'

'And they don't mind?'

'No, I think they were probably quite relieved when I left. They had a lot more peace and quiet.'

'That was what I wanted. There was no peace with my mother around, constantly telling me what to do.'

'It must have been difficult for you.'

'It was. You see my dad died,' Annabel continued. 'I think that's part of the trouble. My mum misses him so much; she's become too dependent on me and thinks she has the right to run my life. She was horrified when I told her I was moving into my own flat.'

'I expect she'll get used to it.'

'That's what everyone says, but I'm not sure. Where did you live before you moved here?'

'I had a flat in London near my office.'

'What made you move to Glentree?'

'Well . . . ' Jack hesitated. 'It's a bit of a long story, but . . . but my girlfriend lived in Glentree and she persuaded me to move into the area.'

I was right, Annabel thought. *He has got a girlfriend*. 'So you lived here with her?' she enquired.

'Oh no. She — Wendy — lived with her parents. I saw an advert in the local paper for someone to share this flat to help pay the rent. I liked the look of it and the rent wasn't too bad, so I moved in.'

'And the person you shared with?'

'He moved out a few weeks ago. He got married; had a whirlwind romance.' Jack smiled. 'Luckily I was promoted at work and got a rise, so I was able to afford the new rent.'

'That was good.'

'Yes, but . . . ' Jack hesitated again. 'Wendy and I split up.'

'Oh, I'm sorry.' Annabel thought she'd better not ask any more questions. She wasn't the only one who had problems with her love life.

'It didn't work out,' Jack continued. 'Wendy just wanted to have fun. She told me she had no intention of settling down for years. If I'd realised that, I probably would never have moved to Glentree — although I really like it here now, and wouldn't want to live in London again.'

'That must have been hard for you.'

'It was at first, but I'm getting over it.' He stopped, looked across at her and said, 'I'm sorry, Anna; why am I boring you with all my troubles? I'm sure that's the last thing you want to hear after a day at work.'

'No, I'm not bored. I'm pleased you can talk to me.'

'That's it, Anna. You're easy to talk to. I shouldn't have taken advantage.'

He thinks I'm easy to talk to, Annabel thought. *That's what I thought about him.* 'You haven't taken advantage,' she replied. 'Talking about your problems can often help.'

'What about you, Anna? Do you have any problems to talk about?'

She grimaced. 'You've met my mother. She's my biggest problem.' *She's one of them,* Annabel thought, *and Garry's another, but I don't think I can talk about him at the moment.*

Jack laughed. 'Yes, I can see that. Anyway, Anna, it's getting dark now. I think it's time to go in, but remember if you need to talk at any time about your mum or anything else, I'm always here. And thank you for listening. I have enjoyed our conversation.'

'Me too,' Annabel replied.

She went inside, thinking her mum was right about one thing: Jack was a very nice man. She was lucky to have someone so pleasant living next door to her.

★ ★ ★

Two days later Annabel decided to ring Garry again. She waited until late in the evening, hoping that he would be home from work. This time he answered the phone immediately.

'Hello, Garry. It's Anna.'

'At last!' he exclaimed. 'I thought you were never going to contact me. Am I pleased to hear your voice! I was beginning to think you'd given up on me.'

'I did ring a few days ago.'

'You did? When?'

'The other evening. You weren't there, and . . . and . . . someone else answered.'

'Someone else? I don't understand.'

'They said you weren't in.'

'It must have been the answer phone.'

'No, Garry. It wasn't that. It . . . it was . . . a woman.'

'A woman?'

'Yes.'

There was a moment's silence, and then Garry replied. 'Oh, of course. I remember now. I was working late. It must have been my sister. She said she was going to come round to do some tidying up for me. She thought my flat had got into a bit of a state. I'd forgotten about that. I didn't see her; she'd gone before I arrived home.'

'Oh.' Annabel didn't know what else to say. His sister? She didn't know he had a sister. He'd never mentioned her before. Was that the truth? Or was he just making it up?

'You've gone very quiet. You do believe me, don't you?'

'I . . . I . . . '

'Anna, I wouldn't lie to you,' Garry interrupted her.

'Wouldn't you? You did before.'

Annabel couldn't resist reminding him of that.

'No, I didn't lie. I just didn't tell you all the facts, but . . . but . . . I thought we'd sorted that out.'

'Had we?'

'Yes, Anna. I'd told you about Chloe and you were going to let me know if you'd forgiven me. Have you?'

'I don't know. I really don't. I thought I had, but then when I telephoned and heard . . . '

'You thought it was my wife, or I was carrying on with some other woman?' Garry said bitterly.

'I didn't know what to think.'

'You trusted me so little?'

'No — er, I'm not sure. The first time I rang you I was going to say I had forgiven you, and was willing to start over again. But when that woman answered I was so shocked — '

'That you thought the worst of me? Is that it? You didn't think there might be some plausible explanation? You imagined me sweet-talking you, and at the same time carrying on with someone else? Or that I was back with my wife? Or maybe you thought I was doing all three — ?' Garry's voice rose to a crescendo. 'Well?'

Annabel was desperately trying to think of a suitable reply. Had she really thought that?

Hearing no response from her, he continued, 'If that's what you think about me, there's not much hope for us, is there? We might as well call it a day now.'

'Oh . . . I . . . I'm . . . '

'Sorry? Is that what you were going to say? I think it's too late for that now, don't you?' His voice was harsh. 'Perhaps we'd better end it all.'

'If that's what you want,' Annabel murmured, feeling tears pricking her eyes. Everything had gone completely wrong. This was not what she'd planned to happen. She'd hoped their misunderstanding would be resolved, but now there seemed to be no chance of that.

'If you have such a low opinion of me, then that's the only option.'

'Garry, I . . . I . . . '

'Don't bother saying anything else,' he interrupted. 'We're finished. Thanks for ringing. Goodbye, Annabel.'

12

'Garry, please listen — ' Annabel begged, but it was too late. He'd hung up. She slammed the phone down and slumped into an armchair, tears of frustration, anger and despair coursing down her cheeks. *It wasn't meant to be like this*, she told herself. *I was going to tell Garry I'd forgiven him and that I wanted us to start again. Why has it all gone so horribly wrong? If only that woman — his sister, if indeed it was his sister — hadn't been in his house at the precise moment I rang. How could one simple incident cause so much trouble? Now what am I going to do?*

Annabel sat for ages replaying in her head the disastrous phone call to Garry. He'd passed judgement on her and hadn't given her a chance to explain how she was feeling. It was all so unfair, but then hadn't she'd jumped to conclusions too? That was what she'd done when she'd heard the woman's voice. Oh, it was such a muddle, and there seemed to be no way out of it. Garry had said he was finished with her. It all sounded so final.

Annabel sat for a long while, alternately sobbing and then feeling convulsed with anger. She hovered between wanting to sort things out with Garry and vowing to have nothing more to do with him. She tried telling herself he wasn't worth all the pain and anguish she'd had in the past few weeks. Perhaps her mother was right — she was better off without him. She'd said it would all end in disaster.

Finally Annabel calmed down, feeling resigned to facing a life without Garry. After all, hadn't she anticipated that, when she'd found out he had a wife? She'd have to make a fresh start and cultivate some new friends. That was her only option now Garry had finally finished with her.

The next day Annabel put her plan into action. She arranged for a couple of the staff to come over in the evening to see her flat. She would not have done this in the days before she knew Garry, she mused, so that was something to thank him for. Previously she hadn't mixed socially with any of the people she worked with; she'd felt too insecure to do so, but since meeting Garry she'd become much more self-confident.

'What a lovely flat!' Brenda exclaimed, sinking into an armchair after having a tour round. 'You were very fortunate finding this one.'

Lynne nodded in agreement as she sat down opposite Brenda. 'And you've made it look really cosy, Anna.'

'Do you think so?'

'Yes I do. You're so lucky to find one as nice as this. Mine's quite grotty compared with yours.'

'Oh I'm sure it's not,' Annabel replied. 'Why don't you come over one evening next week and see for yourself? You too, Brenda. You'll get a shock.'

'I'd love to,' Annabel replied.

'Do you think there are any more of these flats up for rent?' Lynne asked. 'I wouldn't mind one myself.'

'I've no idea, but I could ask my neighbour. He might know.'

'Can we go on the balcony?' Lynne asked. 'That's something else I'd like, a balcony or a terrace.'

'Yes of course we can. It is nice having a balcony, especially in this hot weather. We'll have our coffee there. I'll take some chairs outside. I haven't got round to buying any garden furniture yet. I didn't actually think I'd need any. I wasn't expecting this heatwave to last for so long.'

'It has been an unusually hot summer this year,' Brenda replied.

While they were sitting drinking, Jack strode outside carrying a glass of beer in his hand. He called across, 'Good evening, Anna. It's another fine one.'

'Yes, too good to stay indoors.'

'I won't disturb you. I can see you're busy,' he said as he sat down.

'No that's all right. We're just relaxing after a long day at the supermarket. These are some friends from work.'

'Pleased to meet you all.' He smiled.

'Jack, do you know if there are any other flats up for rent?' Annabel asked.

'I think they're all taken now, but people often come and go, so I'll keep an eye open for you. Who wants to know?'

'I do,' Lynne answered. 'I'm most impressed.'

'Okay, I'll see what I can find out.'

'Thanks,' Lynne replied.

'Well, I'll leave you three ladies in peace. Have a good evening.' Jack picked up a newspaper and started reading.

Later on when they had gone back inside, Lynne said, 'I like your neighbour, Anna. He's a real hunk . . . so good-looking. I wouldn't mind living next to him.'

'Yes, he's a real stunner,' Brenda agreed, 'but a bit too young for me. He's all right for you two though.'

Lynne retorted, 'I don't know about that. A lot of women have toy boys these days.'

The three women laughed. They enjoyed the rest of the evening and arranged that the following week they would all meet at Lynne's flat.

★   ★   ★

One morning a few days later, as Annabel arrived at the supermarket, Daniel came out of his office and called her over. 'I've been hearing such good things about your flat.'

'Oh I suppose Brenda told you.'

'That's right. And Lynne — she was most enthusiastic.'

'Yes, I'm very lucky.'

'I'm so glad everything seems to be working out for you, Annabel. What with the accident and the hard times you had with your mother.'

'Thanks, Daniel. 'What about you? How's everything with you?'

'I'm very well, thank you.'

That wasn't what Annabel had meant. She really wanted to know if he was still with his glamorous girlfriend Olivia, but didn't like to ask.

'I was wondering, Annabel . . . ' Daniel hesitated. 'Is . . . is there any chance I could have a peep at your flat? The girls gave it such a glowing report that I'm curious about it. I wouldn't stay long . . . maybe call in one day on my way home from work. That is, if you don't mind. Er, when it's convenient for you.'

'Of course you can, Daniel. Whenever you like.'

'Tomorrow? I'm free then. What about you?'

'That'll be fine. I haven't got anything arranged.'

'Right, I'll see you at about eight.'

'I'll look forward to it.'

That night Annabel lay in bed reflecting on the events of the past few days. She was beginning to build a social life for herself. She'd really enjoyed entertaining her colleagues from work and was looking forward to visiting Lynne the next week, and now Daniel was going to call in. She thought it was very nice of him to take an interest in what she was doing. It was something she'd never imagined happening. What would her mother say if she found out? She'd think something was going on, but Annabel knew Daniel was just being friendly, as he was with everyone. He was that kind of person, always polite and thoughtful for others. Anyway, he had a girlfriend. Annabel would have to make sure her mum didn't find out, otherwise she'd be sure to say something embarrassing.

Life was definitely getting better, Annabel decided. She was even able to cope with seeing her mother once a week. After her debacle with Garry she'd been in despair, but now she was becoming so busy she wouldn't have time to miss him. She knew that wasn't true, but was trying to convince herself it was. She hadn't heard from Garry since he'd hung up on her and didn't expect to anymore. That episode in her life was well and truly over.

* * *

The next evening Daniel arrived precisely at eight o' clock. He was carrying a pink potted rose in his hand. 'Hello, Annabel. This is for you.'

'Thank you, Daniel. It's beautiful. I'll put in on the windowsill. Have you got time for a drink?'

'That would be lovely, thanks.'

'Come and sit down. Tea, coffee or a cold drink?'

'A glass of orange juice, if you have it, please.' Daniel made himself comfortable on the sofa while Annabel poured him a drink. 'I can see what the girls mean. You've got a very nice flat,' he remarked as he gazed around the room.

'You haven't seen it all yet.'

'No, but I'm sure the rest is just as good.'

'It is.'

'What does your policeman friend

think of it?' Daniel asked.

'We . . . we've split up. He hasn't seen it.'

'Oh, I'm so sorry. I didn't realise. I shouldn't have asked.'

'No, that's all right. Why would you know?'

'Do . . . do you want to talk about it?'

'Not really. I'm getting over it now.' That was a lie, but if she said it often enough, she might even believe it herself. She was also wondering if Daniel was still seeing his glamorous girlfriend, but was too shy to ask. 'I'll show you the rest of the flat,' Annabel said, changing the subject.

After they'd finished looking around, Annabel opened up the door to the balcony and Daniel followed her outside.

'Hi, Anna.'

'Oh, hello, Jack.' She hadn't noticed that he was outside dragging a huge bag of compost to the other end of his balcony.

'I'm doing a spot of gardening,' he called breathlessly.

'So I see.' She smiled.

'I'd better get on,' Jack said, eyeing Daniel. 'I mustn't distract you from your company. I want to finish this before it gets dark.' He turned away and continued lugging the compost.

'Okay. Good night, Jack.'

'What a good view over Glentree!' Daniel remarked as he gazed around.

'Yes it is, and it's lovely to have a bit of outside space,' Annabel replied. 'I don't think I'd like to live in a flat without a balcony. Can I get you another drink?'

'No, thank you. I'll have to get going,' he told her. 'Still got some paperwork to do before I go to bed tonight.'

They walked inside. 'I see you've met your neighbour already,' Daniel commented. 'Looks a nice, young chap.'

'Yes, he is.'

'It's good for you to have other young people around. It'll stop you from being lonely, especially now . . . you . . . aren't with your policeman friend. What are your other neighbours like?'

'I haven't seen much of them. I think they must work long hours and they rarely come out onto their balconies. I don't see Jack often though. Only in the evening, when we tend to go out onto the balcony at the same time to get a bit of fresh air while it's still so hot.'

Annabel felt she had to point this out to Daniel. She didn't want him to think she'd taken up with Jack so soon after finishing with Garry. She was also amused by the way he'd referred to her and Jack as being young, as if he was so much older. She didn't know Daniel's exact age, but guessed he was only about ten years her senior, yet he seemed to be acting in a rather paternal way towards her. Perhaps he'd always seen her in that light and she'd never realised that before. But, she reminded herself, his girlfriend was also a fair bit younger. Maybe because she appeared so sophisticated and self-assured, Daniel didn't think of her as being young. The truth was, Annabel didn't know what he was thinking. She wasn't very good at fathoming men's minds.

* * *

The hot, humid weather continued. Annabel's mother came on another visit and immediately suggested they went outside to eat. 'Why don't you take our dinner onto the balcony? It'll be a lot cooler out there.'

'All right.'

Annabel knew that Maggie was hoping to see Jack again, but she was disappointed this time. There was no sign of him. When they'd finished eating Maggie remarked, 'That neighbour of yours has made his balcony look really nice. Those potted plants are gorgeous. You ought to do something like that. If you ask him, I'm sure he would help you.'

'I haven't had time to worry about decorating my balcony. I've been much too busy. Besides, I've felt too hot to mess around with plant pots and compost.'

She's still trying to match-make me with Jack, Annabel thought, *but she's wasting her time there. I'm not interested in him and he's certainly not interested in me; he hasn't got over his girlfriend leaving.*

'But if I do decide to do something,' Annabel added, 'I won't need to ask Jack. I'll do it myself. I'm quite capable.'

'That's where you play your cards wrong, Annabel. Jack would probably love to help you. You're too independent. That's your trouble.'

'You want me to play the little helpless female?'

'Not exactly, but you need to use some feminine wiles.'

'Like you do,' Annabel muttered to herself.

'What was that you said?'

'Nothing.'

'It's a pity that your neighbour isn't in. Wouldn't have minded having a chat with him; such a nice young man.'

'He's probably still at work or out with friends. I'm sure he's got better things to do than sit around chatting to us.'

'You're probably right. I suppose a good-looking chap like him has a girl-friend. Oh Annabel, you miss out on everything. Your boss is spoken for and I expect Jack is too. All you could find for yourself was that awful pushy policeman, and now he's gone too, thank goodness — and you only met him because he ran you over. I think you're destined to be the eternal spinster.'

'Thanks, mum. You say the nicest things!'

'I just speak as I find.'

'I thought you wanted me to stay single.'

'Well, that was only if you had contin-ued living with me. But now you've moved out, things are different. I quite fancy the idea of becoming a grandmother.'

'You can forget that. It's not going to happen.'

'I think you're right there, worse luck. You're getting a bit too old for that.'

'I'm not too old, but I haven't got a partner.' Annabel's voice rose in indignation. She was wondering if Garry wanted children. She'd never thought of that before. She would have liked children if everything had worked out between them. She'd never heard her mother mention grandchildren before. That was something new. Well, on that count she was going to be unlucky. Life was very hard sometimes, Annabel mused. Then she told herself once again to stop dwelling on the past. Concentrate on the future.

'Sorry, what did you say?' Maggie was droning on and Annabel hadn't heard a word.

'I said it's time we went inside. It's getting a bit chilly now. Don't want to catch a cold; got no one to look after me if I'm ill.'

'Okay, mum. I'll make another coffee and then I'll walk you home before it gets too dark.' Annabel was thinking, *I've got no one to look after me either,* but she didn't say anything.

Two days later she was climbing the stairs to her flat when Jack caught up with her. 'Hi, Anna. How are you?'

'I'm okay thanks,' she replied breathlessly. 'A bit tired. We had so many customers in the store that there were several complaints about the long queues. I think this weather's making everyone short-tempered.'

They reached the landing and stood outside Annabel's front door.

'I'm sure it is. I expect all your customers have been buying ice cream and things for their barbecues. This hot spell seems to be going on and on. There's no respite. We're not used to it. At least I'm in a nice, cool, air-conditioned office. It must be awful for you on your feet all day in this heat.'

'It is, even though we have got air conditioning. You're right about my customers. That's exactly what they're buying. We can't keep up with them,' she sighed. 'It's so hot I can't be bothered to cook anything tonight, so I'm going to make a couple of sandwiches and sit outside.'

'I think I'll do the same. Isn't your boyfriend coming over, Anna?'

'Boyfriend?'

'The chap who was out on the balcony with you the other night?'

'Oh Daniel. He's not my boyfriend. He's my boss.' Annabel smiled.

'I'm sorry. I thought — '

'That's all right,' Annabel interrupted. She felt flattered. At one time she would've loved to have Daniel as her boyfriend, she mused, but now it was still Garry she was pining for, in spite of all her intentions to forget him. 'I'm lucky,' she continued. 'Daniel's a very good boss. He wanted to see the flat.'

'Well, I did think he looked a bit old for you.'

'Old?' Annabel stared at Jack. How old did he think she was? 'I'm not that young.'

'Sorry. I shouldn't have said that. I'm

afraid I keep putting my foot in it. I should keep quiet.'

'Don't worry about it. I do the same.'

'I can't believe that. Anyway, I think I'd better go in before I say something else I shouldn't. Good night, Anna. I might see you outside later.'

'You might.'

Annabel didn't see Jack again that evening. Soon after she had gone inside there was a text on her mobile phone from Garry that put paid to all her good intentions. Annabel wanted to ignore it but her curiosity got the better of her.

'I'm really sorry,' she read. 'I didn't mean what I said. Please don't delete this. Ring me tonight if possible; I am at home. On a very important case; all leave cancelled after tomorrow for a while, till we get the job cleared up. Waiting for your call. Love from Garry.'

Now what was she to do? Annabel wondered. Should she ignore him, or should she reply? She couldn't decide.

13

Annabel sat for a long time staring at her mobile phone, wondering what to do. She'd just started making a new life for herself without Garry, and now his message had brought all the old memories flooding back. Should she ignore his text, or send him a reply? *He doesn't deserve another chance after the way he's treated me*, she reasoned, *but then if I don't answer I might regret it later. I've nothing to lose if I do speak to him again. I can't be any worse off than I am now*, she rationalised, *and I do want to find out what he has to say.* So finally she plucked up courage, picked up her mobile and rang his number.

Immediately Garry answered. 'Annabel, I'm so glad you've rung. I was worried that you wouldn't read my text, or that you'd ignore it. I know I deserve it after the way I treated you, but I get so wound up that I act without thinking.'

Didn't she do the same thing sometimes? After all, that was how she came to have the accident. She'd stepped out into the road without being aware of what she was doing.

'Are you still there, Annabel?' Garry was saying. 'It's gone very quiet.'

'Yes, I'm still here.'

So, do . . . do you think you could forgive me, Annabel? Please say yes.'

'I . . . I don't know.'

'I can understand how you're feeling, but I promise it won't happen again. I won't do anything else to hurt you. What do you say, Annabel? Will you forgive me?' Garry pleaded.

She hesitated. 'I . . . I suppose I could try.'

'Thanks, Annabel. I won't let you down.'

'I'm Anna.'

'I didn't dare call you that. I thought you might be offended.'

'All my friends call me Anna. Only my mother objects, but you know that.'

'Does that mean . . . ? We . . . we're friends again? You'll give me another chance?'

'I said I'll try.'

'Oh Anna, thank you. I wish I could see you, but we've got this wretched case on at work. I don't know when I'll be free again.' He paused. 'I . . . I've just thought, are you at home?'

'I am.'

'Could I come and pick you up . . . maybe take you out for a drink?'

'I . . . I guess so.'

'Can you be ready in an hour? It'll be my last chance to see you for a while. I'll wait outside so I don't have to upset your mother. I know she won't be pleased to see me.'

'No, Garry, you won't have to do that.'

'Why? What do you mean?'

'I . . . I've moved.'

'You've moved?'

'Yes.'

'You don't live with your mother anymore?'

'No.'

'Oh, that's marvellous. It's what you wanted, isn't it? Can I come round to see where you live? I'll be good. I promise. You do believe me?'

'Yes, I believe you,' Annabel confirmed. 'Er . . . why don't you come round here for coffee? We don't have to go out.'

'If you're sure it's not too much trouble.'

'No, of course it's not. I could show you round then.'

'That'll be lovely. Right, what's your address? I'll see you in an hour.'

★ ★ ★

As soon as she'd hung up, Annabel was having mixed feelings about the forthcoming meeting. Should she have given in so easily? Maybe she should have refused to see him. That was what he deserved, she mused. *But then I wouldn't know what excuses he had for his appalling behaviour. Anyway, I've agreed, so I'll have to get on with it.*

Annabel was feeling hot, partly because of the weather, but also because she was stressed out by the phone call. She quickly freshened up and changed into a cool top and skirt. She opened her windows wide but kept the balcony door closed. She didn't want Garry going outside while Jack was there. What would he think if she appeared on the balcony with another man in tow? He'd be wondering what she was up to. Then she told herself, *I don't know why you're fussing over what Jack thinks. He's probably not in the least concerned with what you do. You worry too much about other people.* That had always been her problem: lack of self-esteem. Now was not the time for contemplation, Annabel decided as she brushed her hair. Garry would be there soon and she wasn't ready yet.

Exactly one hour later, Garry rang the doorbell. 'Come in,' she said shyly, stepping back. 'Welcome to my new home.'

He followed her into the lounge. 'This is very nice,' he answered, looking around appreciatively. 'What a lovely flat!'

'That's what everyone says,' she replied. 'Come and sit down.'

'Oh, have you had a lot of people here then?' Garry asked as he made himself comfortable on her sofa.

'No, just a few friends.'

'What about your mother?'

'Yes, she's seen it.'

'Does she like it?'

'She hasn't said much, but I think she does. I'll go and put the kettle on. I won't be a minute.'

'Okay.'

Annabel escaped to the kitchen. Feeling a little dizzy, she clutched the table to steady herself. Was this really happening? Garry was in her flat. This was something she'd been dreaming about for so long, but had feared would never happen. She had to be very careful. One false move and everything could go wrong again. She took a deep breath, made their drinks, placed some biscuits on a tray and carried them into the lounge. She noticed at once the balcony door was wide open.

'That was quick,' Garry said, putting down the house and garden magazine he'd selected from the coffee table. He cleared a space for the tray. 'Been trying to get some ideas?' he asked, pointing to the magazine.

'Yes, I'm not used to all this homemaking. I've never done it before.'

'I suppose not.'

She passed him his coffee 'Help yourself to a biscuit, Garry.'

'Thanks.'

'My mother chose everything, even when my father was alive,' Annabel continued. 'She was always the boss.'

'I can imagine that. But this flat looks so good you don't need to do much to it.'

'No, and I'm glad about that.'

'I hope you don't mind — I opened

up the door to the balcony. It was so hot in here. I needed a bit of air. Saw your neighbour sitting out there; seems a nice friendly chap.'

'What did he say?'

'Nothing much, just that he'd spoken to you a few times.'

'Oh.' Annabel couldn't think of anything else to say. She was wishing it wasn't so hot. She hadn't wanted Garry to see Jack. She knew she was being irrational, but for some reason she thought it would be better to keep her friendship with him apart from Garry. She didn't think Garry was the jealous sort but she didn't want to take any chances. Then she told herself, *What does it matter if they do meet? Jack's just a neighbour, and Garry . . . well . . . I . . . I suppose he's . . . my . . . boyfriend.* She liked the sound of that.

'As I was saying,' Garry continued, 'have you seen what your neighbour's done to his balcony? He's made a really good job of it. Looks a treat.'

'Er, yes I suppose it does.' That was

what her mother had said. 'I'll be glad when this heatwave passes.' Annabel changed the subject. 'It's been unbearable.'

They sat quietly sipping their coffee until Garry stared at her intently, broke the silence and said, 'Well this is all very cosy, Anna, but there's something I've got to ask. Have . . . have you . . . really forgiven me?'

'I . . . ' Annabel hesitated. 'I . . . I suppose so. I told you on the phone I would try.' She seemed to be making a habit of this, she mused. Forgiving Garry.

'I know you did, but I took you by surprise then. I thought you might have had time to change your mind.'

'I don't change that quickly.'

'No. I'm sorry. I shouldn't have said that.'

'You don't have to apologise.'

'Thanks, Anna. I won't upset you again, I promise.'

'That might be a difficult one to keep,' Annabel replied.

'Well, I will try my hardest not to hurt you any more. Is that good enough? Will you give me another chance? Can we start again?'

She couldn't resist his pleading any longer. 'Yes, I . . . '

'We can?' he whooped.

'That's what I said. We — '

Before she had time to finish the sentence, Garry jumped up from the sofa, rushed across the room, pulled her into his arms and kissed her. 'Thank you, Anna,' he breathed. Then he gently lifted her hands and kissed each finger in turn as she gazed at him in wonder. *Sometimes dreams do come true*, she was thinking, *but will it last?*

'I wish I wasn't so busy at work,' Garry was saying. 'I don't know when we can see each other again. There's so much going on these days that they keep cancelling our leave.'

'I suppose it's all these terrorist threats that are causing it. Is that right?'

'Something like that, but I can't say any more.'

'No, of course you can't. I shouldn't have asked.'

'That's all right. As soon as everything gets back to normal I'll be in touch and we'll go out to celebrate.'

'Lovely. What are we celebrating?'

'Us getting back together.'

That sounded wonderful, Annabel mused. What she'd wanted for so long, but thought would never happen. 'Good,' she replied.

'Are you hungry?' Garry asked.

Suddenly she felt ravenous. She remembered she'd told Jack she was going to make some sandwiches, but when she got that text from Garry she'd forgotten about it. 'Yes I am, rather.'

'Well, how about we order a takeaway? I didn't get round to having anything to eat this evening.'

'Neither did I. You look as if you haven't eaten for weeks,' Annabel said, stroking his gaunt face.

'I haven't eaten much. I did lose my appetite. Food was the last thing on my mind, what with work and thinking about ways of winning you back.'

'Oh Garry, I lost my appetite too, but it's come back now with a vengeance. I could eat a horse.'

'I'm starving but I'm not that desperate.' He smiled.

Annabel laughed. 'No, we won't have that. What do you fancy? Pizza, Chinese or Indian?'

'I don't mind. You choose.'

'Pizza and salad.'

'Okay.'

'I'll order it now.'

The rest of the evening passed pleasantly. They both ate heartily, chatting non-stop as if to make up for lost time. They seemed to be back to their old easy relationship, discussing Annabel's job, the heatwave and what was happening in the world in general. Nothing was said about Garry's wife or his marriage. Although Annabel wanted more information, she felt this was not the appropriate time. She would leave it for another occasion, feeling confident now that there would be other opportunities. Garry was very attentive to her, letting her know how much he had missed her and how miserable he'd been. She couldn't resist telling him that he'd been the one to finish everything.

'I know that,' Garry groaned. 'You don't have to remind me. Sometimes I do and say things without thinking and then later on I wish I hadn't.'

'I'm just the same,' Annabel assured him. 'You see, we have that in common.'

'We probably have a lot in common,' Garry replied. 'We like the same kind of music, neither of us are keen on dancing and we both work very hard.'

'That's true.'

'While we're talking about music, do you fancy going to another concert at the college in three weeks? I hope that by then I'll be able to have an evening off work.'

'That sounds lovely. I think I heard somebody at the supermarket talking about it. They're such a good orchestra.'

'Yes, they sound quite professional.

The last concert was excellent. Right, that's a date. I'll do my utmost to keep the evening free. I'll book it in on my next shift.'

'Wonderful.'

'I'm not sure if I'll be able to see you before then.'

'That's a long time.'

'There's nothing I can do about it, but if I can see you I'll let you know. We'll keep in touch. I'll text or ring whenever I can. Anyway, I'm afraid I'll have to go now.'

They walked to the door and Garry put his arms around Annabel, kissed her and said, 'Sleep well, my Belle. Thank you for being so understanding.'

'Good night, Garry. I'll look forward to hearing from you.' She watched and waved as he walked away.

14

Annabel had another sleepless night. This time it was because she was excited about her reconciliation with Garry. She felt it was all like a fairytale, but would there be a happy ending or would it end in disaster once again? she wondered. She would have to be very careful and do everything in her power to prevent that from happening. She knew her mother could cause trouble as she did before, so Annabel decided not to mention Garry to her at the moment. There'd be plenty of time later to do that if things went well. Now she couldn't take the risk of allowing anything to spoil her happiness.

The heatwave continued and when Maggie visited Annabel the next time, she again wanted to go out on the balcony. 'It's so hot. Shall we eat our dinner outside?' she asked.

'I think it's too warm,' Annabel replied. She knew Jack might be there and didn't want her mother to get into a conversation with him, partly because she was prone to saying something embarrassing, or it was possible Jack could even mention Garry. Annabel hadn't had a chance to speak to Jack since he'd spoken to Garry on the balcony while Annabel had been making their drinks.

'No, it's not too warm.' Maggie stomped over to the door. 'It's cooler out there. I'm going, so if you don't join me you'll have to eat alone in here.'

'Okay, if you insist.'

Annabel prepared their meal and the two women sat outside under the sun umbrella, enjoying the food and trying to keep cool.

'Thought we might have seen your neighbour,' Maggie remarked. 'On a nice evening like this, I was sure he'd be out on his balcony.'

'He's probably still at work,' Annabel replied, praying that was the case. She guessed that the main reason her mother wanted to go on the balcony was because she hoped to see Jack. It was not because she was too hot.

'That's a pity. It would have been nice to have a chat with him.'

'You said that the last time you came here.'

'Well, sitting here with no one to talk to can be a bit boring,' Maggie sighed.

'You've got me,' Annabel answered sharply.

'You don't count. I can talk to you at any time.'

'Thanks, Mum. You say the nicest things.'

'There's no need to be sarcastic.'

'Why do you come here then, if you don't want to talk to me?' Annabel retorted.

'Don't get all uppity with me, my girl. I just meant that I could phone you up at any time and have a chat.'

Annabel forced herself to keep quiet. She'd never win with her mother. They were completely incompatible. Moving out was the best thing she'd done. At least she only had to put up with her once a week now.

These thoughts were going through her head when she heard Maggie say, 'Hello, Jack. Nice to see you again. I was saying to Annabel, I wondered if you'd be coming onto your balcony tonight.'

'Oh good evening, Mrs Barker. I've only just got home from work. Hello, Annabel. How's everything?'

'Fine, thank you.' She hoped Jack didn't think they'd come outside especially to see him.

'That's good. Have you — '

'I've been admiring your window boxes,' Maggie interrupted. 'Annabel could do with something like that to brighten up her balcony. Have you got any suggestions?'

'Er . . . I'd be pleased to be of help if . . . if she'd . . . '

'Mum, stop pestering Jack. I'm sure he's very busy and has got better things to do than stand out here gossiping with us.' Annabel glared at her mother.

'No, I don't mind at all. As I was saying, I'd be pleased to offer any assistance . . . ' He turned to Annabel. 'That is if you'd like me to, even if it's just carrying a bag or two of compost up here.'

'That's very kind,' Maggie answered beaming at him. 'See, I told you Jack would help.'

At that moment, to her relief, Annabel's mobile phone sounded. 'If you'll excuse me, I think I'd better answer it,' she said, glancing at Jack, who had an amused expression on his face. 'It could be important. It might be someone from work. They've been quite short-staffed today.'

She went inside, leaving her mother still chatting to Jack. Annabel wasn't really expecting anyone from the supermarket to text her. Instead she was hoping it would be a message from Garry, but she couldn't say that in front of her mother. Besides, if it was from Garry she wanted to read it away from her mother's prying eyes. She hurried inside and grabbed the phone.

She was in luck. It was from Garry. 'Should be free next Tuesday,' she read, 'unless there are any developments on the case. Will pick you up at seven thirty. We'll have dinner together. Text me if that's okay. Love, Garry.'

'Wonderful,' she replied. 'See you then. Love, Anna.'

Suddenly Annabel felt much more cheerful. She'd been annoyed with her mother for trying yet again to match-make her with Jack, but now all she could think of was that she was going to see Garry in a few days.

She went back outside and heard Jack saying, 'It's been nice talking to you, Mrs Barker, but I'll have to go in now and cook my supper. Good night. Enjoy the rest of your evening.' Seeing Annabel approaching, he called, 'I hope it wasn't bad news.'

'No, nothing like that.'

'That's good. Bye, Annabel; see you soon.'

'Sorry about my mother. I hope she hasn't been bothering you,' she mouthed as Maggie clambered out of her chair and made her way to the door.

'Not at all. We just had a pleasant chat.'

He's being polite, Annabel thought as she replied, 'Oh, all right. Good night, Jack.'

'Are you coming?' Maggie called to her daughter. 'Jack's got the right idea. It's getting a bit chilly out here.'

'You look very pleased with yourself,' Annabel remarked when they were back sitting in the lounge.

'I am. I've found out quite a bit of information while you've been on your mobile.'

'Now what have you been saying?'

'Well to start with I've discovered Jack hasn't got a girlfriend, so . . . '

'You didn't ask him that, did you?' Annabel shrieked.

'Why not? At least we know now, so if you play your cards right, you might be in with a chance. I think he likes you.'

'Mum, why do you have to embarrass me?' Annabel wailed. 'I shan't know what to say to him the next time I see him. Anyway, I'm not interested in him; I've told you that before. Why do you keep trying to pair us up? I feel so stupid now.'

'I only want to help. You're not doing a very good job of finding yourself a man, so I'm trying to do it for you.'

'I don't need any help from you.' Annabel glared at her mother. 'For the final time, will you get it into your head — I am not interested in Jack or any other man that you might find.'

'You're so ungrateful. I'm doing my best for you but you don't appreciate anything I do,' Maggie sniffed.

'I'm grown up now. I want to make my own decisions, so please let me get on with my life in my own way,' Annabel said more calmly. She guessed her mother really did think she was helping.

'Oh well, if you want to be an old maid, don't blame me. I've done my best for you, but you've always been a wilful girl, right from when you were a tiny baby,' Maggie complained, glancing across at Annabel. 'I can't see what you've got against Jack. Unless . . . unless you're still holding a torch for that . . . that . . . POLICEMAN.' She spat out the words. When Annabel didn't reply, Maggie groaned, 'Oh no. I do believe you are.'

'I'm not saying another word. The discussion's over,' Annabel said firmly. 'It's about time I took you home. You want to get in before it's dark.'

'You've answered my question,' Maggie muttered. 'I can see it in your face. You're a very silly girl. That policeman doesn't want you. Anyway, he's married. Oh . . . ' She put her hand to her mouth. 'You haven't made it up with him, have you? Surely you can't be that stupid!' Maggie stared at Annabel, who ignored her mother's remark as she started stacking the dishes ready to take into the kitchen. 'Did you hear what I said?'

'I heard, but I told you I'm not discussing it, so you had better change the subject,' Annabel replied through clenched teeth. *Why do I have to listen to this?* she was thinking. *I can't put up with Mum much longer. One day I'll explode and say something terrible. She's like a dog with a bone. She won't give up. She'd try the patience of the Archangel Gabriel himself.*

'You're lucky enough to live next door to a real gentleman,' Maggie continued, seemingly oblivious of Annabel's rising anger. 'And you just don't appreciate it. I've no idea what's to become of you when . . . when I . . . I'm no longer around to keep an eye on you.' Her voice faltered. 'How will . . . ?'

'Mum! You're not yet sixty. You'll be around for years,' Annabel interrupted. 'Stop going all pathetic. I don't need you or anyone else to keep an eye on me, so there's no need to worry. I'll be fine. Now are we going home tonight, or are you staying here? I can make up a bed for you,' Annabel told Maggie, knowing her mother would refuse.

'Not likely. I want to sleep in my own bed. I'm not having you waking me up at some ungodly hour because you've got to go to work.'

★　★　★

The next few days seemed to drag. Annabel couldn't wait for Tuesday to come, when she would be seeing Garry again. He'd said he was taking her out for a meal. She wondered where it would be and pondered what to wear. She'd lost another couple of pounds in weight, which she was very pleased about, and had purchased a new gold satin top decorated with sequins. Would this be suitable, or would she look over-dressed? She'd never have dared to wear something like this when she was living with her mother, partly because she'd have disapproved but also because she was a lot heavier then. She could just imagine what her mother would have said: 'You look like a dog's dinner,' or 'A bit of glitter's not going to improve your looks' was another of her favourite ex-pressions.

Nothing Annabel did ever satisfied her mother; she knew that she'd always been a disappointment to her, but had never understood why. She supposed it was because she was not pretty and petite. She knew her mother had always wanted a delicate, feminine little daughter, and Annabel had never been that. This had made her become very self-conscious about her rather robust figure, and because of this she'd probably not made the best of herself. Her father, however, had always admired her, although he didn't often say it. But Annabel guessed that men saw things differently, especially fathers of daughters. Garry did, too. Hadn't he told her she was pretty? He'd even said she was beautiful. That was an exaggeration, Annabel felt, but nevertheless it was good to hear it. So from now on, she wouldn't worry about what her mother said. She'd do as she pleased. She'd wear that new top with confidence.

On Monday she had a brief text from Garry saying that he was looking forward to the next day. 'I am too,' she replied.

The heatwave was still continuing and Annabel found it very tiring at work on Tuesday. The customers seemed unusually grumpy and even Daniel looked grim.

'We've got to tidy up the shelves,' he kept muttering. 'Look at the state they're in. I don't know what's been going on in here today.'

'Okay. I'll get it sorted,' Annabel promised. 'I expect it's — '

'And make sure they keep that way,' Daniel interrupted, not letting her finish her sentence as he stormed back into his office. 'It's a real shambles in here.'

'I will,' Annabel called after Daniel, feeling somewhat bewildered by his uncustomary ill temper.

She started work on it immediately, thinking that the shelves weren't that bad really, but she didn't want to upset Daniel. She'd been getting on so well with him recently. *Maybe the heat's got to him too*, Annabel thought. When he'd interrupted her she'd been about to say that it was probably the extremely hot weather which was affecting their customers. They were picking things off the shelves to look at and not putting them back in the right places, as well as knocking other items onto the floor and then not bothering to bend down in the heat to pick them up. Annabel felt worn out by the time she had finished bobbing up and down, making everywhere tidy. She could have delegated the job to someone else, but as Daniel had specifically asked her, she decided to do it herself.

Then, just as Annabel was about to leave to go home, she could hear an irate male voice stating, 'It was definitely a twenty-pound note I gave you. What's the idea? Trying to cheat me out of my money? Is that what you're doing? Want to take it for yourself? I suppose they don't pay you enough in here.'

'No, I'm so sorry,' a gentle voice was saying. 'I wouldn't do that. It was a twenty-pound note. You're quite right. I'll just have to call someone senior to open the till for me. Then we can sort it out and I'll give you your correct change.'

'I've no time for this nonsense. Just give it to me now,' the man grunted impatiently.

Annabel thought, *I could have done without this tonight; I wanted to get home early.* She walked over to the counter where one of their new temporary students was looking very upset and flustered.

'Can I help you, Mr Jenkins?' Annabel asked, turning to the elderly man.

'You most certainly can,' he snapped. 'This young lady's trying to cheat me. I gave her a twenty-pound note and she's only given me change for ten. Thank goodness you've come along, Miss Barker.'

'I'm really sorry,' the student replied. 'I realised what I'd done as soon as I closed the till. I was trying to explain to this gentleman that I had to tell a member of the permanent staff, but . . .'

her voice tailed off. 'He wouldn't . . . '

'Now, Mr Jenkins, none of our staff would ever do that,' Annabel said in a calm, silky tone, giving him a big smile.

'Well, I wasn't to know that.'

'This is Leila,' Annabel continued, 'one of our temporary staff who's working here over the summer. It's only her third day. She's admitted her mistake, so no harm's been done, and she did the right thing in asking for help.' Annabel opened the till and turned to the girl. 'Give Mr Jenkins the change, please, Leila.'

'Thanks,' Mr Jenkins muttered ungraciously as he snatched the money from Leila's hands and trudged out of the supermarket.

'I . . . I'm so sorry,' Leila murmured, looking close to tears.

'Don't worry about it. Most of our customers are very nice but there are a few like him. He's harmless really — old and lonely I think, and has probably got overheated. You just concentrate on what you're doing so you won't make the same mistake again.'

'I'll try to be more careful,' Leila promised.

'Good. Now, if there are no more problems, I'll get off home. Brenda's in charge when I'm not here, so if you're worried about anything just ask her.'

'I will, and . . . and thank you for being so kind.'

'That's all right. Good night, Leila.

Annabel walked away feeling glad that everything had been sorted out quite amicably and that Daniel Owen hadn't come along and heard every-thing. After all, Mr Jenkins was one of their most difficult customers and he could have made more fuss. She also felt pleased when Leila thanked her for being kind. That was something which hadn't often been said about her in the past. She'd always found it difficult to relate to the younger staff, but recently she'd found it easier. She guessed it was because she was happier and more confident in herself. She had Garry to thank for that. He'd boosted her confidence no end.

Annabel hurried home. She'd hoped to have time to relax in a long, lingering bath, but that wasn't possible; she was so much later than expected. She rushed around, trying to be ready for when Garry came to collect her. Finally she glanced in the mirror and felt reasonably pleased with her appearance. Her new top fitted well and her brown hair was gleaming.

When seven thirty came, Annabel sat down to get her breath back before Garry arrived. She'd been checking her mobile phone regularly to make sure there were no messages from him to say that he was delayed at work, but there'd been none.

At seven forty-five she was becoming a little anxious about his non-appearance, and at eight o'clock she was extremely worried. She tried ringing but there was no reply, so she sent a text, but again there was no word from Garry. By then she'd convinced herself that she had got the time wrong and he'd come in a few minutes, but there was no sign of him.

When eight thirty arrived she was in a dreadful state, not knowing whether to be upset or angry. Could something have happened to Garry? Had there been an accident? Was he just working late? But if so, why hadn't he contacted her? Or was this his way of finishing with her? Annabel was distraught and didn't know what to think.

15

At nine o'clock Annabel took off her fine clothes and make-up, put on her dressing gown and sat on the bed. She switched on the television and tried to concentrate on watching a light reality programme, but tears kept welling up into her eyes. All the time there was the question running through the back of her mind: had Garry dumped her? Why had he not shown up? Once again she was having negative thoughts about him, whereas only a short time ago she'd felt so positive, believing they were back together and everything would be fine. She'd done nothing wrong. She had trusted Garry, and now that trust was broken. Had she been too forgiving?

If he'd had to work late, surely he could have contacted her? She knew he'd been on some top-secret case, but he'd promised to keep in touch and let her know if he was unable to see her. Garry must have known she'd be worried and upset at him not turning up.

She wouldn't have treated anyone like that. She'd have made sure they knew what was going on. So, the only conclusion she could come to was that he had finished with her. But why? Didn't Garry have the decency to tell her face to face? Did it have something to do with his wife? Maybe she wanted him back. But Garry had said that would never happen; they were getting divorced. *Is that the truth? Can you believe what he said? After all, you know very little about him*, Annabel reminded herself.

Yet logically none of this made any sense. They had been getting on really well, and Garry had genuinely seemed to care for her, so why would he behave so badly and leave her in this quandary?

Annabel alternated between rage and indignation at what he'd done and despair and disbelief that all her hopes for the future had been dashed. She was desperately trying not to cry. Weeks ago she'd sobbed her heart out when she'd first discovered Garry was married and had determined that she wouldn't get herself in such a state again. Anyway, she reasoned, this time was different; she was more angry than upset. He'd led her on, telling her he was going to take her out, and then left her sitting at home all dressed up with nowhere to go. That was outrageous.

Well, Annabel decided, *if he does try to get in touch, he won't con me again. He'll have to come up with some very good excuse this time before I forgive him.*

She switched the television off. It was a waste of time having it on. She'd not seen or heard a thing. Suddenly Annabel realised she was hungry, as she'd had no dinner. She'd been looking forward to having a meal with Garry. It was too late now to cook anything, so she made a bowl of porridge and sat eating that.

She was nearly finished when her telephone rang. That must be Garry, she decided, but was surprised he was ringing the land line and not her mobile. *I'm not going to answer*, she thought. What excuse could he give? Let him wait. But then curiosity got the better of her. Supposing he had a good reason why he couldn't phone? He might have had an accident. Or maybe it wasn't Garry who was ringing. It could be someone from the supermarket with an important message, or even her mother. Perhaps she was ill. Reluctantly, Annabel picked up the receiver. 'Hello?'

'Hello, Anna. This is Jack. I'm sorry to bother you so late, but I've just come in from work and was about to make myself a coffee when I discovered I've got no milk. I know this sounds silly, but I left it out of the fridge this morning and it's gone off. I overslept and was in a rush and must have forgotten to put it back, and in this heat it's gone bad. I was wondering if you had any to spare.'

'Oh . . . er . . . hello, Jack. Yes, I've got a couple of unused cartons.'

'Would you be an angel and let me have one please?'

'Of course, but I'm not very angelic.'

'Well, you will be to me, if you give me some milk.'

In spite of her inner turmoil, Annabel had to smile. 'Okay.'

'Can I come round and collect it?'

'Yes, all right, but could you give me ten minutes?'

'Sorry, am I interrupting something?'

'No, I was just relaxing.' *That's a lie*, she thought. *I'm anything but relaxed.*

'Thanks, Anna. See you in a few minutes then.'

Annabel quickly ate the last few mouthfuls of cereal, put the dish in the sink, washed her face, brushed her hair and put on a skirt and T-shirt. She went into the kitchen and fished a carton of milk from the cupboard. As she was doing so, Jack rang the bell.

She carried the milk to the door. 'Will this be all right?' she asked.

'That'll be fine. You've saved my day. It's been a dreadful one, and coming home finding the milk's gone off was the final straw.'

'Oh, I'm sorry. What happened?'

'Don't ask. It's a long story,' he sighed. 'I won't bore you with it.'

'I don't mind. You can tell me all about it if you want.' Annabel hesitated. 'Why . . . why don't you come in and I'll make you a coffee? That is . . . if . . . you would like to?' Annabel thought, *I might as well have a chat with Jack. I've nothing else to do now Garry's stood me up, and Jack sounds as fed up as I am.*

'I'd love it. Thanks, Anna, but I won't talk about work. It really is too boring.'

'Okay, if you're sure you don't want to get it off your chest. Anyway, come in. I'll put the kettle on.'

Jack followed Annabel into the kitchen. 'Your flat's the mirror image of mine. I thought it would be. It's a lot tidier though.'

'Bare is what I call it. I still need to

get a few things to brighten it up a bit.'

'Like a coffee machine, for example? I use mine all the time ... That is, when I haven't run out of milk.' He smiled.

'Yes, I suppose so. I have a toaster but I haven't got round to choosing one of those yet. There are too many on the market. I don't know which one to buy, so I'm afraid you'll have to put up with instant coffee.'

'That's all right. I'm just grateful for anything tonight. I can show you my coffee machine another day if you like. I think it's brilliant. Even better, I'll give you a demonstration.'

'That would be nice.'

Annabel made their drinks, opened a packet of biscuits and put them on a plate, and Jack helped her to carry everything into the lounge. They were sitting facing each other, drinking and chatting amicably, when Annabel's mobile sounded. She picked it up, glanced at it and saw there was a text from Garry. Suddenly she felt breathless and her heart started racing. What did he have to say? Was he going to make some excuse? She wanted to know but couldn't bring herself to look while Jack was there. She was not sure how she was going to react and she didn't want to embarrass herself in front of him. She hoped Jack hadn't noticed her discomfiture.

'Aren't you going to look at it?' Jack asked. 'I don't mind. I'll just sit here quietly and finish my coffee.'

'No, it can wait.' *Garry can have a taste of his own medicine*, Annabel thought. *I'll keep him dangling. See how he likes it. He probably thinks I'm sitting by my phone longing for it to ring. Well I'm not.*

Ten minutes later there was another text message and again Annabel ignored it, guessing it was from Garry. She wanted to punish him for her ruined evening.

'Don't you think you ought to look at it?' Jack enquired. 'It might be important.'

'No, I expect it's from the phone company offering me something I don't want.' *That's another lie*, she thought. *I'm sure it's from Garry, and it might be very important, but I'm not going to tell Jack that.* 'I get so many of these nuisance calls,' she added.

'Well, I think I'd better be getting back. I've got an early start in the morning. Thanks so much for your help, Anna. You're a star! I'll do the same for you one day. And remember what I said to your mother about helping you assemble furniture. I'm a wizard with flat packs.'

'Don't talk about my mother.' Annabel grimaced. 'The things she says! She's beyond a joke.'

'She's all right,' Jack replied.

'Yes she is to you, but you're not related to her and you haven't had to live with her.'

'No, but she probably means well.' Jack smiled.

'I don't think so. She just takes every opportunity she can to embarrass or humiliate me.'

'I'm sure she doesn't intend to.'

'You don't know her. Anyway, to get back to your offer on assembling flat packs, I'll have to choose something first. I'm not sure what I want yet.'

'Okay. I can help with that too. I've got some catalogues you can borrow.'

'Thanks, Jack. Maybe I'll do that another day.'

'Any time you want anything done, I'm your man. Remember that.'

'I will,' Annabel promised, thinking, *It's not Jack I want to do things for me, it's Garry — but there's not much chance of that. Even if he gives me a good excuse for what happened tonight and we do make it up, we hardly ever see each other; he's always so busy with his work.*

After Annabel had seen Jack off she grabbed her mobile phone, sat down on the sofa and with a thumping heart she read the first message: 'Hi, Anna. Sorry I've messed up your evening. Am on a top-secret job. Can't say any more; will be in touch soon. Please forgive me. Love, Garry.' The second one just said,

'Did you get my text? Am I forgiven?'

Now Annabel felt even more confused. It seemed that Garry genuinely did have to work. So her worst nightmares about him finishing with her were unfounded. That was good, of course, but she couldn't imagine why he was too busy to send a message, to let her know what was happening. Had he just forgotten? Or was he not allowed to contact anyone when he was on a top-secret job? Then it occurred to her that he could be telling lies. After all, hadn't she just lied to Jack? Was Garry seeing somebody else? But then if he was, why would he bother making excuses to her? What could he gain from it? There would be no point in him doing that; he could just finish with her. Annabel was back to square one, so her only option was to give him the benefit of the doubt and see where that led.

She replied, 'We'll see.' That would be sufficient for now. Annabel wasn't going to make it easy for him. He was going to pay for the way he'd treated her. Meanwhile, she had to wait patiently for him to contact her.

Her patience was rewarded the next evening. She had returned from the supermarket after another scorching day and was having a shower trying to get cool when she heard her mobile phone ringing, so she hurried out of the shower, wrapped a towel around herself and picked it up. She was too late; whoever it was had hung up. She scrolled through to find out if there was a voice mail. There was, from Garry.

He said, 'Hi Anna. This is Garry. Can you please ring me? I want to apologise for yesterday. I'll be in all evening waiting for your call. Please take pity on a lonely man.'

Annabel's first reaction was to ignore his call, so he would know how she felt when she'd waited in vain for him to come round or make contact with her. But then she decided that would be a punishment for her as well as him. As usual, her curiosity had got the better of her. She wanted to know what had happened.

She quickly dried herself off, put on her nightclothes, sat down on the sofa and rang Garry's number. He answered immediately. 'Hello, Anna. I'm so glad you've rung me.'

'Are you?' she answered as coolly as she could in spite of her heart racing.

'Of course I am. I wanted to try to explain what happened yesterday.'

'Go on then.'

'You're not making it easy for me.'

'Why should I?'

'You sound so disapproving.'

'I should think so after what you did — leaving me stuck at home all dressed up, ready to go out for a meal. Surely you could have sent a message to let me know what was going on? I was imagining all sorts of things. Had you been in an accident? Had you finished — '

'Anna, listen,' Garry interrupted. 'I couldn't send a message, at least not until later. I hope you weren't about to say that you were wondering if I'd finished with you.'

'Well . . . er, what was I to think?'

'You still don't trust me, do you?'

'It's not that, but . . . '

'I promised I wouldn't hurt you again. I thought you believed me.'

'I did,' Annabel replied. 'But I was confused. When you didn't turn up and there was no message . . . I . . . suppose . . . I . . . thought the worst.'

'Is it always going to be like this?' Garry sighed. 'There's no hope for us if you keep on doubting me.'

'I'm sorry,' Annabel murmured in a little voice.

'We were on a top-secret surveillance mission,' Garry continued, 'and it just wasn't possible to contact anyone. I'm afraid that's what my job is like sometimes. I didn't want to upset you but I couldn't do anything about it. I was looking forward to going out with you. I was disappointed too. Do you think I liked having to work instead of taking you out?'

'No . . . of course not. I just didn't

think.' Annabel felt awful. She'd only seen things from her point of view. She hadn't considered what Garry was feeling.

'So, am I forgiven, Anna?'

16

'What's your answer, Anna?' Garry asked. 'Am I forgiven? I didn't deliberately let you down. I couldn't help it. You do believe me, don't you?'

'Yes, I believe you. I . . . I shouldn't have doubted you. I was so disappointed . . . I wasn't thinking straight. I could only see things from my point of view. I should have realised you had to work.'

'So you forgive me?'

'Of course I do, but really there's nothing to forgive. I'm the one who's in the wrong for not trusting you. I'm so sorry, Garry.' Suddenly Annabel began to feel calmer. All her fears had been groundless.

'But you've nothing to be sorry about, Anna. It was my fault entirely. Thanks for being so understanding. I'll make it up to you.'

'You see,' Annabel continued, 'I was

furious at the time and let my imagina-
tion run away with me. I suppose I'll
have to get used to situations like that
and not . . . think . . . the worst.'

'I'm afraid so. My job has caused a
lot of problems over the years and it
won't ever be much different. If . . . if
we have any future together, Anna, then
you'll have to come to terms with it.
Do you think you could do that?'

'I'll have to.' Annabel liked the sound
of that. Garry was talking about their
future together. It was what she'd been
dreaming about for so long.

'That was partly why Chloe and I
split up,' Garry went on. 'She couldn't
accept the long hours I had to work.
She wanted a husband who would be
there every evening to cosset her and
take her out. I couldn't be that husband.'

'I see.'

'I love my job, Anna. I've wanted to
be a policeman ever since I was a boy. I
can't change now. It's my life.'

'No. I do understand. I don't think I
did before. I'll just have to get used to

not knowing when I'm going to see you.'

'Chloe couldn't do that. I was beginning to think that no one else would either until I met you.'

'I'm sorry it's taken me so long to understand.'

'It hasn't. You've been marvellous.'

'No I haven't, but thank you for saying that.'

'Now we've got that all sorted, are you still able to go to the concert at the college?'

'Yes. I wouldn't want to miss it.'

'Well this week I'll probably be late every night. We're still working on the case, but by Saturday I really should be free.'

'And if you're not?'

'I'll try my hardest to let you know. I'm sorry I can't give you more details, but I'm not allowed to, so that's all I can say.'

'It's all right, Garry. I won't be so paranoid next time you don't turn up on time. I'll know that you really can't help it.'

'Thanks, Anna. I'll see you the night

of the concert then. It's not too far off now. I will try to text you and ring when I can, but if you don't hear, you'll know it's because of my job. It's not that I don't care.'

'Yes, I know that now.'

'Good night, my Belle.'

★ ★ ★

The next week seemed to pass slowly to Annabel. She couldn't wait for the day of the concert to come. Garry sent a few brief texts to say he was missing her and she replied saying the same. He kept assuring her that this time he would be able to come. He'd booked it in with his boss to have that evening off, no matter what crisis or catastrophe occurred in the country.

Two days before the concert Annabel was eating her dinner out on the balcony when Jack came out to water his plants. 'Hello, Anna.' He put down his watering can. 'When's this heatwave going to end?'

'At the weekend I think, but they don't always get it right. It has gone on for a long while though. We desperately need some rain.'

'Don't I know it? Every night I have to come out and do this. Let's hope it will rain in the evening then.'

'Why? Are you doing something special at the weekend?'

'I am actually. I'm glad I've seen you. I wanted to ask you something. I'm going to the concert at the college and . . . I have a spare ticket and I . . . wondered if . . . if you would like to go. That is, if you're not doing anything.'

'Oh I'm sorry, Jack. I . . . I'm going already.' Annabel hadn't expected Jack to ask her this.

'That's all right, but if . . . if you're going on your own . . . '

'I will be with someone, or at least I should be,' Annabel interrupted, guessing he was going to suggest they go together.

'Oh, I should have known.'

'Why should you?'

'I suppose it's that chap I saw on your balcony last week. Oh sorry, Anna; there I go again, putting my foot in it. I shouldn't have said that. It's none of my business who you go with.'

'You don't have to apologise. As I've said before, I do the same thing sometimes — speak without thinking. Yes you did see Garry on the balcony. He was admiring your plants. Garry's . . . my . . . my boyfriend; he's a policeman. He should be off duty then.' Annabel felt she had to say that. She hadn't anticipated Jack asking her to go out with him. She didn't want any more complications in her life.

'I should have realised a pretty girl like you would have a boyfriend. I won't ask you again. I don't want to cause any trouble. Good night, Anna, and enjoy the concert on Saturday.' He picked up his watering can and walked inside, leaving Annabel feeling awkward and uncomfortable. She was just glad that her mum wasn't there to witness Jack asking her to go out with him. It was

261

what her mother had wanted. She'd said that she thought Jack was interested in her. Annabel had dismissed the idea, but maybe her mum had been right for once.

Annabel couldn't help feeling flattered that Jack had called her a pretty girl. She still wasn't used to receiving so many compliments. *It must be because I've lost weight and changed my hairstyle*, Annabel decided. She also wondered whether Jack would still go to the concert on Saturday — and if he did, whether he would go alone or with someone else.

★　★　★

Saturday came at last, and so did the rain. Annabel went to the hairdresser in the morning and was glad of the protection of her big umbrella. She felt pleased with the way her hair looked. It was shoulder-length with just the right amount of curl. While it was being blow-dried she sat happily imagining the evening she was going to have with Garry. He'd sent her a text that morning to say he would definitely be available no matter what, even if some major catastrophe was to hit the country. She knew now that she'd forgiven Garry and believed that he'd told her the truth. She would have to build up her trust in him again. He genuinely seemed as happy as she was at their reconciliation, so Annabel decided not to let any bad thoughts spoil the day.

It was raining even harder when she left the hairdresser's, but fortunately the umbrella was big enough to keep her hair dry.

Garry arrived exactly on time that evening. 'Anna, you look wonderful,' he gasped as she opened the front door to him. 'So slim and elegant. That black dress really suits you.'

Annabel blushed with pleasure. She was glad that she had purchased the new long satin dress. Recently she'd had several compliments about her svelte figure and was determined to keep it.

She had hesitated in the shop before making the purchase, as she could hear her mother's voice in her head saying, 'What do you want to wear black for? You're not going to a funeral, are you? And that dress is far too tight. Do you want to make a spectacle of yourself?'

The sales girl in the department store had assured her that the dress wasn't too tight. 'It fits you perfectly,' she'd said.

Annabel's mother had never liked black, but Garry did. Some time ago he'd suggested that she bought herself a black dress.

'And your hair, Anna,' Garry was saying. 'I love that style. You look a million dollars.'

Secretly Annabel was thinking, *Garry's going a bit over the top*, but she didn't mind. *At least he's noticed that I've made an effort for him*. She guessed he was trying to make up for upsetting her.

Garry had parked very close to the flat so Annabel didn't get wet when she climbed into his car. She sat back as if in a dream, watching the rain running down the windscreen as Garry drove carefully along the wet roads. They were back together again, she kept thinking. But would everything be all right this time? She prayed it would.

Soon they arrived at the college and Garry found a parking space close to the main door. 'It's a good thing we got here early,' he remarked. 'I don't want you getting wet and spoiling your beautiful outfit and hairstyle. It's a terrible night. A bit of a shock after all that fine weather.'

'No, I didn't expect it either. We're too used to the sunshine.'

Garry held the umbrella over Annabel as they hurried into the college.

'I'll just freshen up,' she told him when they got inside. She walked into the ladies' cloakroom and was astonished to see Lynne, one of her colleagues from the supermarket, brushing herself down and looking extremely wet and bedraggled. 'Whatever's happened to you?' Annabel asked.

'I tripped over.'

'I can see that. Are you hurt?'

'Just a bit. My leg was bleeding but I think it's stopped now.'

'Let me have a look.'

Lynne pushed her wet, muddied skirt aside and Annabel could see a nasty gash on her knee. 'Let me clean it up. You don't want it to become infected.'

'No, I can manage, thanks.' Lynne dabbed it with a tissue and winced.

'Are you on your own?'

'I'm with my boyfriend John. He's waiting outside.'

'That's good. Are you quite sure you don't want my help?'

'I ... I don't think so. I feel so stupid. I hate being a nuisance.'

Annabel could see tears welling up in Lynne's eyes. 'Let me help you. You're not a nuisance. It's lethal outside. Anyone could have had an accident ... all those puddles and wet leaves everywhere. Sit down and I'll clean it up for you. I've got some antiseptic cream in my bag. Been carrying it around since my accident.'

'Oh, that's very kind of you.'

'Shall I give your dress a wipe too? It's badly spattered with mud.'

'Thanks, Anna. You've saved my day.'

Ten minutes later Lynne looked much more presentable and she hobbled off back to her boyfriend while Annabel went to find Garry. 'Where have you been?' he asked. 'I was about to send out a search party for you.'

'I had to help a . . . a friend from the supermarket who'd fallen over in the mud.' Yes, Lynne was a friend, Annabel thought. She couldn't have said that a few months ago though. Now she knew how to relate to her staff, and it was all thanks to Garry and her newfound self-confidence.

'So you've done your good deed for the day.' He broke into her reverie.

'I suppose so.'

'Is she all right?'

'Yes, I think she is now.'

'Well, it was really slippery out there. That's why I held on to you so tightly.

Didn't want you having another accident.'

'No. One was enough, although . . . ' Annabel hesitated.

'Although what?' Garry asked.

'Well, if I hadn't had the accident I wouldn't have — '

'Met me. Was that what you were going to say?'

'Yes, and my life wouldn't have changed so much.'

'Ah, now is that a good thing?'

'That would be telling.' Annabel smiled. 'I'll let you know another day. Do you think we ought to go and find our seats?' She changed the subject.

'Okay.'

They climbed up to the balcony and made themselves comfortable. Garry purchased a programme and perused it while Annabel looked around. Suddenly she tugged his arm. 'Look down there.' She pointed.

'What am I looking at?'

'It's my boss, Daniel, and his girl-friend. Look at that dress. It's stunning.

It must have cost a fortune. I wonder where he met her.'

'Oh no, not him again! He seems to follow us around. I reckon half of the staff from your supermarket are here tonight,' Garry sighed. 'We don't have to go and chat with him in the interval, do we?'

'I shouldn't think so. I expect he wants to be alone with his girlfriend.'

'Good. I know the feeling. What about the one who fell over? Have we got to go and talk to her?'

'No. She wouldn't want that, I'm sure. After all, I am her supervisor. I'm probably the last person she wanted to see, especially as she was so bedraggled.'

'I hope we don't see anyone else we know,' Garry remarked. 'I was looking forward to an evening alone with you.'

'I've been looking forward to it too, but I suppose Glentree isn't that big a place. It's not surprising we bump into people we know, especially at the college. These concerts are very popular.'

'I guess you're right.'

'What about your colleagues?' Annabel asked. 'Have you seen anyone from the police station?'

'No, and we're not likely to either. They'll all be working. I had to ask for a special favour from my boss to get tonight off.'

'Did you really? Thanks, Garry.' Annabel took hold of his hand.

Garry gently kissed her fingers. 'Well, I've hardly had any leave recently, and I didn't want you getting upset like the last time when I didn't turn up. I think we have had enough misunderstandings, don't you?'

'More than enough.' She smiled as Garry clasped her hand.

The lights dimmed and they settled back into their seats ready to enjoy the concert, when somebody clambered past the people at the end of the row and squeezed past Annabel.

'Excuse me,' he whispered. 'So sorry to disturb you. Oh . . . er, hello, Anna.'

'Jack!' she exclaimed as he sank down into the seat next to Garry.

17

'How nice to see you,' Jack murmured as Annabel and Garry sank back into their seats.

'That's your neighbour, isn't it?' Garry whispered as Jack made himself comfortable next to him.

'Yes,' she replied.

'Did you know he was going to be here?'

'No — er, not really.'

'What does that mean?'

Annabel was spared from answering as the music started. How embarrassing, she thought, and what a coincidence that out of all the seats in the auditorium, he should have the one next to Garry! There was a spare seat on the other side. So he hadn't found anyone to go with him, she mused. *I was hoping we wouldn't see Jack — or if we did, he'd be with someone.*

Annabel felt ill at ease and worried about what Garry might be thinking. He'd said he was looking forward to being alone with her, and she was sure that sitting next to Jack was the last thing he wanted. She hoped Jack would be tactful and not try to monopolise them during the interval. Annabel didn't think Garry was the jealous type, but she didn't know him all that well and couldn't predict what might be going through his mind. When he said he hoped they wouldn't see anyone else they knew, should she have told Garry that Jack might be there?

Annabel was feeling quite unsettled. She'd wanted this evening to be perfect, but now she wasn't sure what was going to happen. She glanced at Garry, who was staring straight ahead, seemingly engrossed in the music. She shifted slightly and placed her hand on the arm of the seat, hoping that Garry would take it in his, but he didn't. Normally this was music that Annabel enjoyed, but because of her anxious state of mind, the overture seemed to drone on and on.

Finally it came to an end and everyone applauded. Garry turned to her and said, 'That was brilliant, wasn't it? This orchestra's so good.'

'Er . . . yes,' she mumbled.

She could see that Jack was clapping enthusiastically too. She leaned back in her seat so as not to catch his eye, praying that he wouldn't try to talk to them. Her prayer was answered. A young man seated just along from Jack had leaned across to him, and they were engaged in conversation.

'Are you enjoying the concert?' Garry asked. 'You seem a little distracted. You're not bothered by your neighbour being here, are you?' he whispered in her ear.

'No, of course not.' *Now why should Garry say that?* Annabel wondered. *I am feeling edgy because Jack's here, and because he'd asked me to go to the concert with him and I'd refused, but I was hoping my embarrassment didn't show.*

'Yes, the music's very good,' Annabel replied with as much enthusiasm as she could muster. 'I'm just a little tired, that's all. Been working hard this week, on the computer and sorting out the stock at the supermarket.'

Garry took her hand in his and squeezed it. 'Oh. I was getting worried that you didn't like the music. I'm glad you are enjoying it.'

Annabel felt better. She relaxed and sat back as the second work started, feeling relieved that Garry seemed to have accepted her explanation.

When the interval came Jack went off on his own, allowing Garry and Annabel to be alone together. The rest of the concert passed uneventfully. They didn't bump into anyone else they knew, even when they left the building to return home.

'Will you come in for a coffee?' Annabel asked as they pulled up outside her flat.

'Yes please, I'd love one,' Garry replied. 'It'll be nice to get out of this rain.' They went inside and Garry followed Annabel into the kitchen. He watched as she prepared their drinks. 'You've made it so cosy here, Anna. You must be very pleased with it.'

'I am.'

'Is your mother getting used to you being here?'

'I think she's resigned to it now. I'm sure it's good for her to be on her own. She's not old, and quite capable of doing things for herself instead of expecting me to do everything for her.'

'It'll probably give her a new lease of life. You never know, she might even find herself a new man.'

'That would be a miracle,' Annabel laughed.

'Would you mind if she did?'

'No, I'd be delighted, but I can't see that happening somehow.'

'You might be surprised. Anyway, that's enough talk about your mother. Let me carry the tray for you.' They went into the lounge. Garry placed their drinks on the table. 'Come and sit next to me, Anna.'

She sat beside him and immediately he started kissing her and stroking her hair. 'You look so lovely tonight, my Belle.'

At first Annabel responded tentatively, thinking, *Should I be doing this? Can I really trust Garry again?*

'Don't be shy, Anna,' he said, mistaking her diffidence for shyness.

'I . . . I'm not shy. I . . . I was just thinking — ' Before she could finish he kissed her again, and this time Annabel couldn't resist.

'There, that's more like it,' he murmured, finally releasing her. 'We'd better drink our coffee before it gets cold.'

As Annabel picked up her cup, her hands wouldn't stop shaking. Garry noticed her trembling fingers. He took hold of them and gently kissed each one in turn. 'You're not nervous of me, are you, Anna?' he asked. 'You're quite safe with me. I won't do anything you don't want.'

'No, I'm not nervous, just very happy.'

Half an hour later Garry got ready to leave. 'I don't want to outstay my welcome. Thank you for a wonderful evening. I'll be in touch as soon as I can. Good night, my Belle. Sleep well,' he whispered as he stroked her hair.

Annabel stood up and escorted him to the door. She watched and waved as he walked away. Then she went inside, switched on the television and tried to watch a film, until finally at three o'clock she decided to go to bed, where she dozed fitfully for a few hours.

The next morning Annabel felt very glad that she didn't have to go to work. She spent the day lazing around her flat, checking her mobile every little while in case there was a message from Garry, but there was none.

When she returned to work, Annabel was shocked to receive a telephone call from Daniel Owen saying that his father had been taken very seriously ill and was in hospital. 'I'm sorry to burden you with this only a short time after your accident, but I've no choice,' Daniel had said. 'I'll need to take some time off to be at his bedside. I know I can rely on you, Anna, to make sure everything runs smoothly while I'm away.'

'Of course I will, Daniel. I'll be glad to look after the store. Don't you concern yourself about a thing. Stay with your dad as long as he needs you.'

'He's not actually conscious,' Daniel told her, 'but I want to be there when he . . . if he wakes up. He's had a stroke. His wife's beside herself with worry. She's not very good in a crisis, so that's why I feel I have to be there. She needs my support almost as much as he does.'

'You go to the hospital. We'll cope. I'm sure your dad will get better. You'll see. He's a strong man,' Annabel tried to reassure Daniel. 'The doctors in the hospital are brilliant. It's amazing what they can do these days.'

'I hope you're right.'

'I am. Anyway, Daniel, stop worrying. I'll keep you informed about how the business is going.'

'Thanks, Anna. I don't know how I'd manage without you.' She flushed with pleasure, thinking it was nice to be appreciated. That was something she didn't get from her mother.

Annabel informed the staff about what had happened and everyone was willing to pull their weight, work longer hours if necessary, and help in any way they could.

'After all,' Brenda had said, 'Daniel's a very good, understanding boss to us, so helping him out when he needs it is the least we can do.'

However, Annabel's mother was not so co-operative. 'You aren't working more hours, are you?' she grumbled when Annabel telephoned and explained that she would be late in collecting her for her weekly visit to the flat. 'As I've said before, they take advantage of you at that supermarket. Can't someone else do the overtime?'

'We're all putting in extra hours,' Annabel told her.

'What about me?' she complained. 'I

need my tea at a set time. I can't wait till late.'

'Why don't you have something to eat first, before I pick you up?' Annabel suggested, trying to be patient.

'Oh, so now you can't be bothered to cook anything for me, even one day a week?'

'No, Mother; I didn't say that. I just thought it might be better for you to eat earlier before I leave work, as you like your meals at regular times. But if you can wait, I'll make your favourite, shepherd's pie.'

'Don't bother,' Maggie snapped. 'I'll do something for myself. Are you sure you want me to come round at all?'

'Of course I do. Please, Mother, try to be a little more sympathetic. Poor Daniel's father is seriously ill in hospital. He's had a stroke. He might even die, and all you can do is moan about who's going to cook your tea.'

'He's that bad?'

'I'm not sure, but Daniel sounded really worried.'

'I remember Mr. Owen senior. He used to come into the supermarket. He was a real gentleman. Shame about what's happened.'

'Yes, it is. Now are you coming round to the flat?'

'All right. You collect me on your way home from work. I'll make myself a snack first, but you can still cook the shepherd's pie.'

'Okay, Mum,' Annabel sighed.

★　　★　　★

When Annabel escorted her mother to the flat on her next visit, the weather had turned very warm again. As before, Maggie huffed and puffed all the way, muttering to herself, 'Why you had to move, I can't imagine. You had a lovely room in my house. Wasn't it good enough for you?'

Annabel ignored her, pretending she hadn't heard. She was tired after all the extra work at the supermarket and didn't want to get involved in an argument.

When they'd finished eating, Maggie suggested they take their drinks onto the balcony. 'We might see your nice neighbour,' she said.

'It's too hot,' Annabel protested. She hadn't seen Jack since the night of the concert and didn't want to get into conversation with him while her mother was present. She still felt embarrassed about having to reject his offer of taking her out and then finding that she and Garry were seated so close to him at the concert. She was also worried that her mum might start match-making again. She knew that for some inexplicable reason, Maggie had taken a liking to Jack.

'No, it's not too hot,' her mother replied, opening the balcony door. 'I'm going outside. I need some air.'

Annabel followed reluctantly, praying that Jack wouldn't be there. But a few minutes later he came out and started erecting a sun umbrella.

'Ooh, hello,' Maggie called. 'I said to Annabel, I wondered if you would be coming out. It's such a lovely evening. Just got home from work, have you?'

'Er . . . yes. Good evening, Mrs Barker. It is very warm. Hello, Annabel. How are you?'

'I'm very well, thank you,' she replied, thinking, *Please don't say anything about the concert.*

'The weather's certainly a lot better than it was the other evening,' Jack stated, turning to Annabel. 'I nearly got drowned coming home from the concert. It was a good programme though. I'm glad I went.'

'That sounds interesting. You've been to a concert? Where was it?' Maggie asked.

'At the college. Didn't Annabel tell you about it?'

'No, she didn't. She was there? Oh . . . do you mean . . . you two went together?' Maggie looked hopefully from one to the other. Then she added, 'Annabel never tells me anything.'

'It was a really good concert. No, I went on my own. Annabel was with her — '

'Have another biscuit, Mum,' Annabel interrupted, glaring at Jack and willing him to be quiet. But he didn't seem to notice.

'Thanks.' Maggie bit into the biscuit, a thoughtful expression on her face. 'So if you didn't go with Annabel, who did?'

'It's not important. Stop bothering Jack. I'm sure he's got better things to do than to waste time chatting with us,' Annabel said, looking imploringly at him.

'No, I'm not too busy,' he said. 'Just glad to get some fresh air and relax for a while.'

'You're a man after my own heart,' Maggie informed him. 'I love being outside. I had to persuade Annabel to come out here. She said it would be too hot, but I knew it wouldn't. I can't see much point in her having a balcony if she doesn't use it. Don't you agree, Jack?'

'She comes out quite a lot, Mrs Barker.' He defended Annabel, who was thinking, *This is just what I thought would happen.*

'Oh, does she?' Maggie stared at her daughter. 'She didn't give me that impression.'

'I am here, you know. I can speak for myself,' Annabel fumed.

'Sorry. I didn't mean to upset you,' Jack apologised.

'I'd like another coffee,' Maggie said, handing her cup over to Annabel. 'Can you make it for me please, dear?'

'Okay, Annabel sighed. 'Won't be a minute.' She walked in thinking, *That's an act she's putting on for Jack's benefit. She never calls me 'dear'. I hope they change the topic of conversation while I'm gone.* She kept the door open so she could hear what was being said while she was waiting for the kettle to boil.

As soon as her daughter had disappeared out of sight, Maggie turned to Jack and asked, 'Who did Annabel go to the concert with?'

'It's none of my business, Mrs Barker.'

'You can tell me. I'm Annabel's mother. We don't have any secrets.'

'I don't know who he was.'

'He? A man?'

'Oh, Mrs Barker.' Jack put his hand to his mouth. 'I've said too much. Please don't ask me any more. I'll say good night. I'd better go in now and get my dinner.' He walked inside and closed the door.

This was just what she feared would happen, Annabel thought. Now there was going to be more trouble from her mother. She'd tricked Jack into revealing more than he'd intended. She took a deep breath, picked up the cup of coffee and carried it outside, waiting for her mother's outburst.

'Thanks. Now perhaps you'll tell me who the man was you went to the concert with.'

'Mum, it's really no concern of yours. I'm grown up now. I can do what I like and go out with whom I please, so don't keep pestering me.'

'You've answered my question.'

'What do you mean?'

'You've got a boyfriend. I knew it! Who is it, Annabel? You're not back with that awful policeman again, are you?'

18

As Annabel tried to sleep that night, she kept remembering the incident on the balcony. It was unfortunate that Jack had come home while she and her mother were still outside.

'So, who is your boyfriend?' Maggie had repeated. 'Is it that policeman, or have you picked up some other bloke?'

'I'm not saying,' Annabel answered.

'Why not? I am your mother.'

'Yes, and I have a right to a private life without having to answer your questions all the time. Who I go out with is my business. Now, let's change the subject before one of us says something we will regret.'

'Don't you snap at me. You're so rude, Annabel.'

'I'm not rude. I'm just trying to be patient. I think you forget that I'm not a little girl any more.'

'And I'm just trying to help you. That's what mothers do. They offer advice.'

'But I don't have to take it. I must make my own decisions.'

'It is that policeman, isn't it?' Maggie persisted.

Finally Annabel gave in. 'Yes, if you must know, Garry and I are back together. Now can we talk about something else please?'

'You'll regret it, my girl. No good will come from it. You'll see.'

'That's enough, Mum.'

Her mother wanted to prolong the conversation but Annabel would say no more. Later as they walked back to Maggie's house she'd said, 'You made a big mistake, not getting involved with Jack. He's such a nice young man. I'm sure he likes you. You'd have done well for yourself there.'

'I told you before I'm not interested in Jack.'

'Or what about your boss, Daniel?' Maggie continued. 'He's a charming man, but it seems you missed out there too. If what you say is true, he's found himself a girlfriend.'

'That's right, he has.'

Maggie sighed. 'I can't understand you. I really can't.'

You never could, Annabel was thinking.

'That Garry won't be here when I come next week, will he?' she asked.

'No, Mum. I'll make sure of that. I don't see him very often. He has to work long hours.'

'Good. I won't come if he's here, I'm telling you straight.'

'No, you'll have me all to yourself,' Annabel assured her.

* * *

The staff at Glentree Supermarket were very pleased when Daniel Owen returned to work a few days later. 'My father's responding well to treatment,' he told Annabel. 'It was touch and go at first. We didn't know what the outcome would be, but now the doctors are quite confident he will make a very good recovery.'

'That's wonderful.'

'It will be a long haul, though.'

'Not too long, I hope,' Annabel replied.

'We'll have to see. His wife's so relieved he's making good progress now. She was in a terrible state at first. She's a lot younger than him and not used to coping with illness. That was why I had to spend so much time at the hospital. It was to support her as well as him.'

Annabel felt pleased that Daniel was confiding in her. 'I'm sure she'll cope,' Annabel assured him. 'She's probably tougher than you think.'

'You might be right. I hope so. Anyway, you've done a brilliant job at keeping everything going while I've been off work,' Daniel told her.

'Brenda helped and we've all been doing extra shifts,' Annabel pointed out.

'Yes, but you organised them all. I'm very grateful to you.'

Annabel could feel herself blushing. It was nice to receive compliments, she thought, especially from her boss. She never got any from her mother though. It would be a miracle if she ever did. She'd telephoned Annabel the day before, on the pretext of asking which shift she would be on, when she next visited. Annabel knew that in reality she was checking up, trying to find out if Garry was there. He was busy working on another top secret case and they hadn't been able to meet since the day of the concert. She'd had a few brief messages from him but that was all.

Then two days later, she received a text saying, 'Can we go out for dinner tonight? I've got a few hours off. Love from Garry.'

Without hesitating, Annabel agreed, thinking, *I must make sure I'm not late leaving work.*

She hurried home and was fumbling in her bag trying to find her key when she saw Jack, who'd arrived back at the same time.

'Hello, Anna. Have you finished work early too?'

'Yes, for once.' She put the key in the lock. She didn't want to get into a long conversation with Jack now. She needed to get herself ready for her date with Garry.

Jack didn't seem to be in any hurry. He stood facing her. 'I was determined not to stay late tonight. I've done more than enough overtime recently. Thought I'd make myself a salad and take it out onto the balcony. Have a relaxing evening. What about you? Is that what you're going to do?'

'No, I — '

Before she had a chance to finish the sentence Jack said, 'I wanted to see you. Wasn't it a coincidence, us having seats close together at the concert the other evening? I hope you don't think I arranged it. I'd no idea that would happen. I didn't want to cause trouble with your boyfriend. He wasn't annoyed, was he?'

Annabel turned the key and opened the door. 'Garry didn't mind. Why should he?'

'No reason . . . I suppose. It's not as if we've ever been out together . . . although your mum got the wrong idea the other evening. Sorry if I said too much.'

'That's all right. I — '

'I wanted to apologise,' Jack interrupted. 'I guess your mum didn't know about your boyfriend, and I had to open my big mouth and give the game away. So sorry, Anna. I hope I haven't made things difficult for you. That's the last thing I want to do.'

'Apology accepted. Now, Jack, I really must go.'

'Oh, am I delaying you? I didn't realise. You should have stopped me.'

'That's okay. Bye, Jack. See you soon.'

Annabel walked into her flat and closed the door before Jack could prolong the conversation. She felt mean for rushing off when he obviously wanted someone to talk to. She knew what that felt like, but this was not the night for it. She guessed Jack was still missing his ex-girlfriend, but that was no concern of hers. Now she had to get ready for her date with Garry.

Annabel looked at her watch. She didn't have very long; she'd have to rush. She quickly had a shower and put on the new sequinned lilac top she'd purchased the previous week. Before losing weight, she would never have had the confidence to wear such a close-fitting garment. She knew her mother wouldn't have approved, but Annabel didn't care. She liked it and hoped Garry would too.

'You're getting too thin,' her mum had said once again, the last time she saw her. 'You look quite scraggy. A girl needs a bit of fat on her. All skin and bones. That's what you are.'

Annabel knew that wasn't true. She'd never been skinny in her life. Whatever she looked like, her mother would criticise. Before, she'd been told she was too fat. Nothing about her daughter would ever satisfy Maggie. Well, there was nothing Annabel could do about that, so she'd given up trying to please her. Now Garry had come into her life, she'd stopped worrying about what her mum said and was concentrating on pleasing him.

Garry arrived punctually at seven o'clock, casually dressed in navy trousers and a blue open-necked shirt. 'You look gorgeous, Anna,' he gasped as he put his arms around her. 'What a beautiful top! It suits you perfectly.' He kissed her and then stroked her hair, which was glinting in the sunlight. 'Your hair's lovely,' he murmured as he kissed her again.

Annabel was glad she had purchased the top and persevered with her diet. She forgot all her anxieties about her mother. She felt young, slim and attractive. This was a new experience for her and she was enjoying every second. Life was wonderful and she was going to enjoy the evening ahead.

As they were driving along, Garry's

mood seemed to change. Suddenly he said, 'It was a bit of a coincidence, your neighbour having a seat next to me at the concert the other evening, wasn't it?'

'Yes, it was.'

'Do you think he planned it?'

'No, of course not. He was as surprised as us.'

'Oh, so you've spoken to him about it?'

'He mentioned it to me.'

'So you've seen him since the concert?'

'He does live next door to me, Garry. I bumped into him this evening, if you must know.'

'I think he's interested in you.'

That was what her mum had said, Annabel thought. And he had invited her to go out with him. But she wasn't interested in him. It was only Garry for her. She replied, 'No, he's just a bit lonely. He's split up with his girlfriend.'

'You seem to know a lot about him.'

'Well he likes to have a chat some-times when we're both on the balcony at the same time.'

'And that's all there is to it?'

'Yes. I'm not interested in him, if that's what you're wondering.' Annabel thought, *Garry's jealous.*

'Good. That's all I wanted to know.'

'Can we forget about Jack, please, Garry?'

'I won't mention him again if you don't.'

Soon they arrived at a smart country inn where Garry had booked a table for them. They sat in the corner of a conservatory restaurant overlooking a small lake. Ducks and geese were cavorting around, making the most of the evening sunshine.

As they ate their meal, the sun went down across the sky in a red and gold haze. Annabel was dazzled by it and by Garry, who seemed to have got over his jealous feelings and was back to his charming self, being very attentive towards her. She was thinking, *I've been waiting for this for so long. No matter what else happens, I will remember this evening for the rest of my life*. At the back of her mind though, there was still this nagging feeling which, however hard she tried to dismiss it, wouldn't go away. *Is this all too good to be true? Can it last? Do Garry and I have a future together?*

'You look pensive,' he remarked. 'Are you all right?'

'Yes, I'm just very happy,' Annabel replied. She couldn't tell Garry what she'd been thinking. He'd say she didn't trust him. Besides, she didn't know what his intentions were towards her.

'Good. That's what I want . . . to make you happy.' Garry smiled.

At the end of the meal as they were sipping their coffee, Annabel said, 'That was delicious, but I'll have to go back on my diet tomorrow.'

'You don't need to diet, Anna. You're just right as you are.'

'Thank you, Garry,' she replied, blushing and looking straight into his eyes.

'What are you staring at?' he asked.

She laughed. 'I was checking up to see if you were wearing contact lenses.

You seem to be seeing me through rose-tinted spectacles.'

'I don't think you realise how attractive you are, Anna. Don't always denigrate yourself.'

'If you'd lived with my mother as long as I have, you'd understand why. She never has a good word to say about me. Everything I do is wrong.'

'You're not living with your mother anymore, thankfully, so forget about what she says. I like you just the way you are.'

'Garry, you're making me feel embarrassed.'

'You shouldn't be. It's time you received some compliments. I've seen the way you've blossomed since you had the accident. I just wish I hadn't caused you so much pain, both from your injuries and also mentally because I didn't tell you about Chloe. Have you forgiven me yet, Anna?'

'You know I have, Garry. But it was a terrible shock finding out like that at the party. I'd not suspected a thing. I couldn't take it all in. I wanted to run away and hide.'

'I'm so sorry, Anna, but can we put it all behind us now . . . make a new start?'

'Yes, of course we can.'

'Good.' Garry squeezed her hand across the table. 'And I won't keep asking you about Jack. You've told me he's just a friend and I believe you, so there's no need for me to be jealous.'

He's admitted he was jealous, Annabel was thinking. How strange! She'd never experienced anything like this before. Could all this be happening to plain Annabel Barker? 'No, there's nothing to be jealous of,' she replied.

'Now all that's out of the way, there's something I'd like to tell you.'

Annabel looked up at Garry and frowned, trying to fathom out his expression, but his face was inscrutable. 'What is it?' she asked hesitantly. Were all her hopes going to be dashed once again?

19

'What is it?' Annabel repeated anxiously, staring at Garry. 'Please tell me.' She was thinking, *Yes, put me out of my misery. Let's get this over with.* Just when she'd believed things were going well, he was looking so solemn. Surely there were no more skeletons in the closet. Or worse still, he wasn't going to end everything, was he? Not after all they'd been through. Please . . . not that!

'Don't look so worried, Anna. It's nothing bad.' He squeezed her hands reassuringly.

'It's not?'

'No, in fact it's good news.'

'Oh.' She stared up at him expectantly.

'Yes, I heard today that my divorce has come through. I'm a free man, Anna. What do you say about that?'

'I . . . I . . . er . . . ' Annabel was speechless. This was the last thing she had expected.

'Aren't you going to congratulate me?'

'Oh, er . . . yes, of course. Congratulations, Garry.'

'Thanks, Anna. You are pleased for me, aren't you?'

'Of course. I . . . I'm just surprised.'

'But I did tell you I was waiting for it to come through.'

Yes he had told her, and she'd believed him, but there'd always been that niggling doubt in her mind, fuelled by her mother's rampant opposition to Garry. Now she knew he'd been speaking the truth when he'd said he was getting a divorce. She'd proved her mother wrong about that.

'I was hoping you'd be as ecstatic as I am,' Garry continued, looking anxiously at her, waiting for a reply.

'Oh, I . . . I am. I'm delighted.' But what would all this signify for them? Annabel was wondering. How would their relationship be different? Did this mean . . . ?

'Now I can take you out without feeling guilty, knowing that I'm free to do so,' Garry cut into her train of thought.

'Yes, I suppose you can.' But was that all it meant to him? Was he not thinking about anything more permanent? Had she been naïve in hoping for that?

'I think this calls for a celebration,' Garry was saying.

'You're right. It does.'

'It's too late now,' he observed looking at his watch. 'We've both got to go to work in the morning, but what about Friday night? I'm off duty then. Can you meet me?'

'Er . . . My mum was coming round then, but I could change it. Maybe she could come tomorrow instead. I'll have to think up some excuse, but she won't be pleased.'

'We could leave it till Saturday if you'd prefer.'

'No. Let's celebrate on Friday. I've

given in too much to my mother over the years. It's time I did what I wanted.'

'Well said, Anna.'

'I'll ring my mum now.'

'If you're sure.'

'I am.'

Annabel took her mobile phone from her bag, tapped the keys and waited.

'Is she not there?' Garry asked.

'She must be home. My mother doesn't go anywhere. She always takes her time to answer. Crawls to the phone . . . Hello, Mum. How are you?' Annabel settled back in her chair. 'Oh, your legs are bad . . . Have you taken anything? . . . Good . . . I'm all right, thanks . . . Sorry, Mum, but I won't be able to see you on Friday. Something's . . . er, come up . . . at work . . . No, it's nothing to worry about . . . What about you coming round tomorrow instead? Sorry it's short notice . . . You'll come? Lovely . . . No, it will just be the two of us . . . Okay, I'll pick you up after work. See you then. Bye, Mum.' Annabel put her phone back into her bag. 'That was easier than I thought. She didn't make as much fuss as I'd anticipated.'

'She's not so bad,' Garry remarked. 'You just have to be firm with her.'

'You don't know her as well as I do. She can be unbearable.'

'Well, I'll just have to work my charm on her.'

'That might be hard.'

'Thanks.' Garry laughed. 'You're so complimentary.'

'I meant she's a difficult case.' Annabel smiled. She was thinking, *Garry's charm hasn't worked so far. Will it ever?* 'Anyway, that's enough talk about my mother. Would you like to come round to my flat on Friday, or would you prefer to go out to celebrate?'

'Let's meet at your flat. I'll bring the champagne.'

'I mustn't drink too much, though, or be late, as I'm on the early shift on Saturday.'

'Okay, Anna. I won't get you drunk or keep you up.'

'Shall I get us something nice to eat?'

'That would be lovely. Thanks, Anna. It will be a night to remember.'

'I hope so.'

'That's settled then. And now I'd better take you home.'

★ ★ ★

Two hours later Annabel lay in bed trying to sleep, but her mind was far too active. She kept drifting back to the events of the evening. She'd had a roller coaster of emotions, feeling elated one moment and despondent the next, believing she was reading too much into the situation. She hoped that now Garry was divorced their relationship would be on a firmer footing, but she still didn't know if that was what he wanted. Was he serious about her, or just enjoying stringing her along? After all, if he was free, he didn't have to stick to just taking her out. He could have his pick of women — younger and much more attractive ones. But he had called her beautiful, she argued. Maybe he said that to any woman he went out with. He'd never actually told her he loved her, but then neither had she told him. Perhaps she'd find out on Friday evening. It was all going to come to a climax then, she was sure.

After he'd kissed her good night, he'd stated, 'It's time we had a good talk. We'll do that on Friday.'

What did that mean? She'd wondered. 'What do we need to talk about?' she'd asked.

'Our future, of course. Can we talk about that, Anna?'

* * *

Maggie visited her daughter as planned. It was a dull, wet evening so they were unable to go out onto the balcony, for which Annabel was thankful.

'What a shame we can't go outside,' Maggie had remarked.

'Never mind. There's a good film on the television. Thought you might like to see that. I'll bring in some trays and

308

we can watch it at the same time as having our dinner. I've made a shepherd's pie.'

'That sounds nice. How's your boss's dad? Is he still ill? Was that why you had to change our plans?'

'Yes, I've been very busy at the supermarket.' Annabel replied, evading the question. 'Daniel's dad is still very ill, but I think he will recover.'

'Oh, I hope so.'

Maggie became engrossed in the film, so there was little time for conversation, and the evening passed off uneventfully.

* * *

The following day Annabel could hardly contain herself waiting for the evening to come. What was Garry going to say? Were all her dreams going to come true? Surely he wouldn't be so cruel as to finish everything? That was too terrible to contemplate.

Daniel was back at work, which was a good thing, Annabel thought, as they were extremely busy. The weather was fine once again and everyone seemed to be purchasing food for their barbecues. Annabel had to supervise the young staff, who were constantly having to replenish the shelves.

After lunch Daniel called her into his office. 'We've made a good profit recently. You all worked so hard while I was off, I think you deserve a bonus. When I have some spare time I'll get it sorted. My accountant's coming over next week so I'll discuss it with him.'

'That'll be lovely.'

'You can tell everyone, Anna. You've all done a brilliant job. I'm so lucky to have such good staff.'

'It works both ways,' Annabel answered. 'You've been good to all of us too.'

'Well, I've tried to follow in my father's footsteps. I think he was always fair to everyone.'

'Yes, he was. How is he now?' Annabel enquired.

'Doing very well. It's such a relief for us, especially his wife. She was beside herself with worry. Anna, I don't want to impose on you as you've worked so hard recently, but can I leave you in charge tonight as I . . . I really need to leave early?'

'Oh, er . . . Are you visiting your dad?' Annabel hesitated, not knowing how to answer. She'd intended to leave early herself to get ready for Garry's visit, but she didn't want to upset her boss if he was going to see his sick father.

'No, not tonight. Actually I've arranged to take Olivia to the theatre. It's her birthday.'

'I see.' Now what could she say? She didn't want to disappoint Daniel, but if she stayed late she wouldn't be ready for Garry and his celebration. So Daniel's romance was going well. That was good. He deserved to be happy.

'Is it all right if I rush off tonight?' he repeated.

'Yes, of course.' She couldn't refuse, especially as Daniel had talked about giving her a bonus.

'Thanks, Anna. I won't forget this.'

'I . . . I hope you have a nice time. What are you going to see?'

'*Macbeth*. Olivia's never seen a Shakespeare play. She's from America, you know.'

'Well, I'm sure she'll enjoy it.'

'I knew I could rely on you.'

'That's okay, Daniel.'

When Annabel left his office she quickly sent a text to Garry saying she had to work late and wouldn't be able to prepare a meal. He should understand, she thought. He was always having to change arrangements because of his job. She just hoped that he'd have time to look at his phone and would see the message. If he didn't they would have to order a take-away.

One hour later she received a reply. 'I'm very busy too. Shall we leave it until tomorrow? We could go out to eat if you like. It will save you having to prepare anything. Love, Garry.'

Now I'll be kept in suspense until tomorrow, Annabel thought. *That's assuming Garry won't have to work then.* Being a policeman's girlfriend wasn't easy, she decided.

Later, as Annabel was entering her flat, Jack arrived home too. 'Hello, Anna,' he called. 'How's everything? Going out tonight, are you?'

'No. Having a night in. Need a rest. Been very busy at the supermarket.'

'I'm tired too, but I'm off out tomorrow for lunch.'

'Anywhere nice?'

'Don't laugh, but I've joined an internet dating agency and I'm meeting my first date.'

'Oh, that's interesting. I hope it works out for you and you have a good time.'

'I'm tired of being on my own so I thought I'd give it a go. How's it going with your boyfriend?'

'Okay, I think.'

'You think?'

'Well, we seem to be getting on well, but he's a policeman and has to work long hours, so it's difficult making plans. But we should be going out tomorrow to celebrate.'

'What are you celebrating?'

'His divorce has come through.' Now why was she telling all this to Jack? It was nothing to do with him, but she'd always found him so easy to talk to.

'I didn't realise.'

'There was no reason why you should.'

'Does your mum know he's been married before?'

'She guessed.'

'I bet she wasn't very happy about it.'

'No, she was horrified. That's part of the reason why she gives me such a hard time. She doesn't like Garry at all. Oh, sorry, Jack. I shouldn't be telling you all my problems.'

'I've told you mine. That's what friends are for, to help each other. And it does help having someone to talk to.'

'That's true.'

'Anyway, as long as you and Garry are happy that's the important thing.' Jack put the key into his lock. 'So tomorrow could be a special day for both of us then . . . a new start.'

'You're right, Jack.'

'Good night, Anna, and the best of luck.'

'Thanks, Jack, and the same to you.'

Annabel walked into her flat thinking that all three of them were at a crossroads. What would the next day bring? Would it be good or bad?

20

The next evening Garry arrived at Annabel's flat at the agreed time. 'Wow!' he gasped as she opened the door. 'You look beautiful, Anna.'

'Thank you,' she replied, thinking, *No one apart from Garry has ever said that*, although secretly she felt he was exaggerating. She was glad she'd made a special effort to look nice but didn't feel she deserved so much praise. She still saw herself as a plain Jane. Now, Garry really did look stunning in his smart navy suit, she thought, but she was too shy to tell him that.

He gave her a brief kiss on the cheek and they set off in his car. 'I've booked us a table,' he told her. Garry concentrated on driving round the winding country lanes while Annabel enjoyed looking out of the window at the scenery.

Fifteen minutes later they arrived at

a country inn. The waiter led them to a secluded alcove overlooking a pleasant garden where roses were blooming in abundance. Garry ordered a glass each of champagne as promised and said, 'Let's drink a toast to celebrate getting my divorce.'

The food was good and the waiter attentive. They talked about work and things in general, but Garry never mentioned the future. *Has he changed his mind?* Annabel wondered. Then finally when they were sipping coffee and munching on after-dinner mints, he said, 'It's time we talked about our future, Anna.'

'Is it?'

'Yes. We can't go on like this for much longer.'

'Can't we? Why not?' What did that mean? Was he going to end it, after all? Annabel looked down so Garry wouldn't see the tears which were stinging her eyes.

'Because it isn't very satisfactory for either of us.'

'I'm not complaining,' she murmured.

'No, you're very patient, Anna, but I'm not. I want a more permanent relationship.'

'You do?' Annabel blinked the tears from her eyes and gazed up at him. What was he saying?

'Yes. We're both very busy people and never know when we are going to see each other . . . so . . . '

'We can't do much about that,' Annabel interrupted him. 'Neither of us want to change our jobs.'

'Can you please let me finish, Anna?' Garry took hold of her hand across the table. 'I know I treated you badly, not telling you about Chloe, and I regret that very much. But you've told me you've forgiven me, and I believe you . . . '

'So . . . ' Annabel stared at him. 'What are you trying to say, Garry?'

'That I . . . I've fallen in love with you and I was wondering if . . . if you felt the same way?'

Was he really saying this? Could this be true, or was she asleep and dreaming?

'Anna, did you hear me?'

'Yes, Garry.' Annabel pulled herself together.

'And your answer?'

'I . . . I do love you.'

'You do? You did say you love me?'

'I did.'

Garry whooped with joy. 'Oh Anna, my Belle.' He picked up her hand and kissed it. 'That was the answer I longed for, but wasn't sure I would get. I probably don't deserve your love . . . '

'I think I have been in love with you since we first met,' Annabel continued, 'but I wasn't sure about your feelings. I was so worried that you were going to finish with me.'

'How could you think that? I love you, Anna.'

'I know that now, but I didn't then.'

'I think I fell in love with you when you were still in hospital looking so fragile after what I'd done to you, but I hardly dared hope you could ever feel the same way.' Garry leaned across the table and kissed her.

Annabel felt so happy she didn't care who was watching. She was also amused that Garry saw her as fragile. That was not a word she would ever have used to describe herself. *They say love is blind*, she mused.

Garry released her when he became aware of the waiter hovering at the end of their table. 'Excuse me, sir, but can I get you anything else?'

'Two more coffees, please.'

'I'll be right back.'

'There's one more thing, Anna.'

'What's that?'

Garry put his hand in his pocket and pulled something out. He held out a square box to Annabel. 'I'd like you to have this as a token of my love and as a peace offering.'

She took it from him and with trembling fingers opened it up, revealing a golden necklace encrusted with diamonds and opals.

'It's beautiful,' she breathed.

'It belonged to my grandmother. My mother was having a sort-out a few weeks ago and she found it and gave it to me. She told me that I should keep it until I fell in love again, and then pass it on to — '

'Your coffees, sir.' The waiter returned and placed them on the table.

'I've never seen anything so lovely.' Annabel couldn't take her eyes off it.

'I've been holding on to it, hoping that I would find the right moment to give it to you. And this seems to be it.'

'Doesn't your mother want it?'

'No. She said Gran would have wanted me to have it. Some people don't like opals . . . they think they're unlucky, but my Gran loved them and she had a very happy life.'

'That's just an old wives' tale. I've always liked opals; they're beautiful.'

'And so are you, my Belle.'

'Oh Garry, I'm so happy.' Annabel leaned across the table and kissed him. 'Thank you. I feel as if I am in a dream.'

'No, this is real, Anna.' He kissed her again to prove it. 'I'm very happy too. After Chloe I didn't know if I would be again, but then I met you and everything changed.'

'It did for me too. I know it sounds funny, but the accident was the best thing that ever happened to me.'

'Well, there's just one thing left to do.'

'What's that?'

He took hold of her hand and gazed anxiously into her eyes. 'Will you marry me, Anna?'

Her eyes filled with tears of joy. All her dreams had come true. 'Yes, Garry. I will,' she whispered.

They kissed across the table. Then he produced another box from his jacket pocket. 'Will you accept this matching ring, Anna? I was waiting to see if you liked the necklace. My granddad gave it to my gran when they got engaged.'

Annabel carefully opened the box and gasped when she saw the ring. 'It's so beautiful,' she murmured as the tears poured down her cheeks.

'What's the matter?' Garry asked in concern.

'I . . . I'm just so happy. I don't know what to say.'

'That's what I want — for you to be happy. Try the ring on. If it doesn't fit we can get it altered. Let me put it on your finger.'

With faltering hands she passed the box to Garry and he placed it on the fourth finger of her left hand. 'There, it fits perfectly,' he said.

She gazed at the large opal surrounded by tiny diamonds. 'Thank you so much, Garry. I can't believe this is happening. You've made me the happiest girl in the world.'

'And I'm the luckiest guy.'

They kissed once more. 'Now we've got a lot of planning to do,' he said as he released her. 'What do you say to a New Year's wedding? We've still got a few months to arrange it.'

'That would be wonderful. I can't wait to show my ring to everyone at work. There's just one problem though.' Annabel's face clouded over.

'I know what that is.'

'You do?'

'Your mother.'

'That's right. I don't think she will be pleased. In fact she will probably be really hostile.'

'Maybe at first, but once the children come along, I'm sure she'll accept it.'

'Children?' Annabel blushed.

'You do want children? I know we haven't talked about it before but I assumed you would want them. I think that was part of the trouble between Chloe and me. She didn't like children.'

'Yes I do want them, but I . . . I never thought it would happen.'

'Everything's going to work out fine, Anna.'

'I hope you're right.'

'I'm a policeman. I'm always right.'

Annabel laughed as she looked around the restaurant. 'I think we'd better go home. Everyone else seems to have gone.'

★   ★   ★

When Annabel went back to work she wore her engagement ring and it was noticed immediately. They all admired it and were delighted for her.

'When's the wedding?' Brenda asked.

'It's not definite, but probably at the beginning of January.'

'That's lovely. A brand new year and a new start.'

'That's what we thought.'

'Have you told your mother?'

'No, not yet. I'm dreading doing it.'

'Why? She should be pleased that her only daughter is getting married.'

'I don't think she will see it like that.'

'She might be happier than you think.'

'I hope you're right.' Annabel was quite sure her mother would be most unhappy about it, but didn't want to discuss it then.

Daniel Owen came out of his office. 'What's all the excitement?' he asked. 'I can hear so much chatter and noise. It's a good job we're not open yet.'

'It's Annabel,' Brenda replied. 'She's got engaged.'

'Really? That's wonderful. Congratulations. Let me see your ring.' She held out her hand. 'That's really beautiful, Anna. I hope you and your fiancé will be very happy.' He kissed her on the cheek. 'It's lovely to hear such good news.'

'It's your turn next, Daniel,' Brenda said slyly.

'Oh, I don't know about that. It's early days for me.' He looked at his watch. 'Now I think you'd all better get to your counters. It's nearly time to let the customers in.'

'Okay, Boss.' Brenda grinned. 'Come on, everyone.'

★ ★ ★

That night as Annabel returned home from the supermarket she bumped into Jack, who was just coming out of his flat. 'Hello, Anna,' he called. 'How's everything? You look very chirpy.'

'I am.' She smiled.

'I guess your love life must be going well then.' Jack looked her up and down, suddenly becoming aware of the ring which was gleaming on her finger. 'Oho . . . what's that I spy? An engagement ring? No wonder you look so happy.' He took hold of her hand and whistled. 'That's some ring. It's beautiful, Anna.'

'I know. I can't believe how lucky I am. Yes, Garry and I are engaged.'

'Congratulations. I hope everything will go well for you.'

'Thanks, Jack.'

'What does your mum think about it?'

'I haven't told her yet. I've still got that pleasure to come.'

'She should be happy for you.'

'I don't think she will be. For some reason she's taken a dislike to Garry.'

'Oh, that's a shame. Maybe she'll get over it when she knows him better.'

'That's what I'm hoping.'

Even now Annabel found herself confiding in Jack. 'Anyway, that's enough about me. How are you?' She glanced at Jack. She'd noticed he was looking unusually smart. 'You seem quite cheerful yourself.

I like your suit. Going somewhere nice?'

'I am, actually . . . got a date with a really gorgeous girl.'

'Oh, I'm so pleased for you.'

'Yes, things are beginning to look up.'

'I hope it will work out for you too.'

'I have a feeling that it will this time. Bye, Anna. I'd better get going. Don't want to be late.'

★ ★ ★

Two days later Annabel collected Maggie and took her to the flat. She'd removed her ring, having decided to wait until after they'd eaten before breaking the news.

When she'd cleared up the meal, Annabel took the plunge. *After all*, she reasoned, *I've got to tell Mum some time.* She put on the ring, made some coffee, took it into the lounge and sat down opposite her mother.

Maggie quickly spotted it. 'What's hat you've got on your finger?' she sped. 'Let me see.'

Annabel held out her hand.

'It's not an . . . an — '

'Yes, Mother. It's an engagement ring,' Annabel interrupted.

'Oh no!' Maggie exploded. 'You silly girl! What have you done? Who . . . who gave it to you?'

Annabel took a deep breath. 'Garry, of course.'

'Garry? That . . . that awful policeman!' she screeched. 'You hardly know him. How could you be so stupid? I thought you'd get over all that nonsense. Anyway, he's a married man. You can't marry him.'

'He was married, Mother, but his divorce has come through.'

'That's what he tells you. You don't believe that, do you? You're so naïve, Annabel.'

'Yes I do believe him, and we're planning on getting married at the beginning of January.'

'So soon? You're making a terrible

mistake, Annabel.' Maggie's face contorted with rage. 'He'll bring you nothing but trouble. Oh . . . you . . . you're . . . ' She put her hand to her mouth.

'What are you trying to say, Mum?'

'You're not . . . pregnant, are you?'

'No I'm not, but I am going to marry Garry whatever you say.'

'You'll live to regret it, my girl. You'll see. It won't work out. He's obviously not suited to marriage. If his first marriage ended in divorce, why will his second be any different?'

'Because we'll make it work. So you might as well get used to the idea.' Annabel wondered where all her courage had come from. She didn't usually stand up to her mother.

'Let me see the ring.'

Annabel held out her hand as her mother scrutinised it and groaned, 'Whatever made you choose an opal?'

'I didn't choose it. Garry gave it to me. It belonged to his grandmother.'

'So he didn't even spend any money on you?'

'I think it's beautiful and very romantic to have a ring that belonged to his grandmother. It still looks like new after all these years. It's worth a fortune. He's given me a matching necklace as well.'

'Don't you know that opals are unlucky?'

'That's just superstition. I don't believe in all that. Besides, Garry's grandmother was very happily married.'

'You'll be sorry. Mark my words. Where are you going to live?'

'Garry will be moving in with me after the wedding, and then we'll look around for a house.'

'Hasn't he got a house already?'

'No, he's been renting, the same as me.'

'Well, don't expect me to come around any more. I don't want to see him.'

'That's your choice, but you'll be the lonely one. So you won't come to our wedding?'

'I . . . I . . . didn't say that.'

'Well, if you come to our wedding

you'll have to see Garry.'

'I suppose I could for once.'

'Don't strain yourself, Mother.'

'There's no need to be sarcastic. I
. . . I . . . just don't want to make a
habit of seeing him.'

Annabel shook her head. Her mother
was impossible.

'You . . . you can . . . still come round
to my house, though,' Maggie sniffed,
'just as long as you don't bring HIM
with you.'

'If that's the way you want it.'

'It is. What about Jack? You silly girl,
missing your chance there. I don't think
he will be very pleased about your
news. Have you told him?'

'Yes, he knows.'

'So everyone seems to have found out
before me. Surely your mother should
have been the first person you told?'

'Jack noticed my ring as I came home
from work.'

'What did he say? I bet he wasn't
very pleased.'

'I think he was.'

'Why do you say that? I think he fancied you.'

'Whether he did or he didn't, Jack will be okay.'

'How do you know?'

'He's joined a dating agency.'

'What?'

'You know, an online marriage bureau.'

'So I was right. He was interested in you. I knew it.'

'We don't know that, Mum. He could have joined for any number of reasons.'

'The poor chap.'

'You don't need to feel sorry for him.'

'Why not?'

'Because he's already got himself a date lined up and he says it's looking very promising.'

'He's a fast worker,' Maggie sniffed. 'Not like in my day. Men were gentlemen then.'

'I've heard all this before. Times have changed, Mum. Now, will you please try to be happy for me?'

'I suppose I've got no choice.'

'No, you haven't.'

'You're so stubborn, Annabel. You make life difficult for everyone. You always have to have the last word. Still, you've made your decision, so you will have to take the consequences. There's nothing more I can say.'

'No, that's right. My mind's made up. Now can we please talk about something else?'

Gradually Maggie calmed down. When it was time for her to leave she said, 'You can come round to my house next week for your supper. I'll cook you something nice.'

'If you're sure it's not too much bother.'

'No, I'll enjoy doing it.'

Now this was something new, Annabel thought — her mother wanting to cook a meal for her!

* * *

That night as Annabel lay in bed thinking back over the evening, she wondered why Maggie had had a sudden change of heart. Was it because this was the first time in her life Annabel had really stood up to her? Once she'd made it clear that she wasn't going to take any notice of anything her mother said, Maggie had backed down. Annabel guessed that if she'd done this sooner, life would have been a lot easier. Perhaps in time her mum would get to like Garry, especially when the children came along. But even if she didn't, Annabel mused, she was looking forward to a future which could only get brighter and better.

THE END

We do hope that you have enjoyed reading this large print book.

Did you know that all of our titles are available for purchase?

We publish a wide range of high quality large print books including:
Romances, Mysteries, Classics
General Fiction
Non Fiction and Westerns

Special interest titles available in large print are:
The Little Oxford Dictionary
Music Book, Song Book
Hymn Book, Service Book

Also available from us courtesy of Oxford University Press:
Young Readers' Dictionary
(large print edition)
Young Readers' Thesaurus
(large print edition)

For further information or a free brochure, please contact us at:
Ulverscroft Large Print Books Ltd.,
The Green, Bradgate Road, Anstey,
Leicester, LE7 7FU, England.
Tel: (00 44) **0116 236 4325**
Fax: (00 44) **0116 234 0205**

Other titles in the
Linford Romance Library:

GIRL WITH A GOLD WING

Jill Barry

It's the 1960s, and Cora Murray dreams of taking to the skies — so when her father shows her a recruitment advertisement for air hostesses, she jumps at the chance to apply. Passing the interview with flying colours, she throws herself into her training, where she is quite literally swept off her feet by First Officer Ross Anderson. But whilst Ross is charming and flirtatious, he's also engaged — and Cora's former boyfriend Dave is intent on regaining her affections . . .

THE SURGEON'S MISTAKE

Chrissie Loveday

Matti Harper has been in love with Ian Faulkner since their school days. He is now an eminent cardiac surgeon, she his theatre nurse. Ian has finally fallen in love — the trouble is, it's with Matti's flatmate Lori! But whilst a heartbroken Matti prepares to be their bridesmaid, Lori is being suspiciously flirtatious with another man. How can Matti tell Ian without appearing to be jealous? Best man Sam Grayling tries to help, but only succeeds in sending things from bad to worse . . .